THE IMMORTALITY WARS

THE
PENITENT

PART II

A. KEITH CARREIRO

COPPER
BEECH
PRESS

First Stillwater River Publications Edition 2019.

ISBN-10: 1-950339-27-0
ISBN-13: 978-1-950339-27-3

1 2 3 4 5 6 7 8 9 10
Written by A. Keith Carreiro.
Cover art by Hollis Michaela. www.hollismichaela.com
Published by Stillwater River Publications, Pawtucket, RI, USA.

Publisher's Cataloging-In-Publication Data
(Prepared by The Donohue Group, Inc.)

    Names: Carreiro, A. Keith, author.
    Title: The Penitent. Part II / A. Keith Carreiro.
    Description: First Stillwater River Publications edition. | Pawtucket, RI, USA :
        Stillwater River Publications, 2019. | Series: The immortality wars
    Identifiers: ISBN 9781950339273 | ISBN 1950339270
    Subjects: LCSH: Orphans--Fiction. | Good and evil--Fiction. | Clairvoyants--
        Fiction. | Soul mates--Fiction. | Speculative fiction. | GSAFD: Christian
        fiction. | LCGFT: Allegories. | Fantasy fiction.
    Classification: LCC PS3603.A774375 P462 2019 | DDC 813/.6--dc23

**Connect with Keith on his website
or other social media platforms:**

https://immortalitywars.com
https://www.facebook.com/keith.carreiro.33
https://instagram.com/immortalitywars/
https://twitter.com/immortalitywars
https://www.linkedin.com/in/keith-carreiro-5040aa17/
https://www.goodreads.com/author/show/15959901
https://reedsy.com/author/a-keith-carreiro

To the storytellers in our lives...

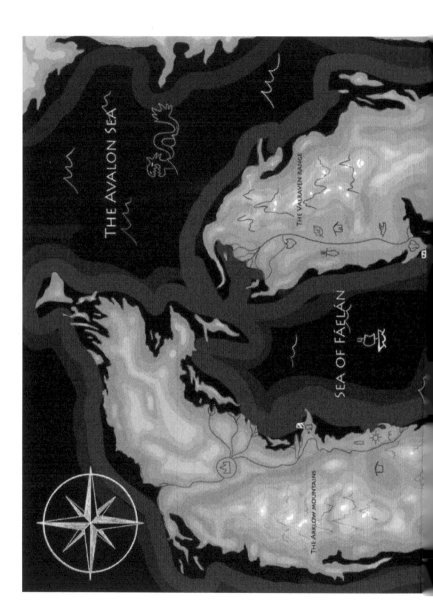

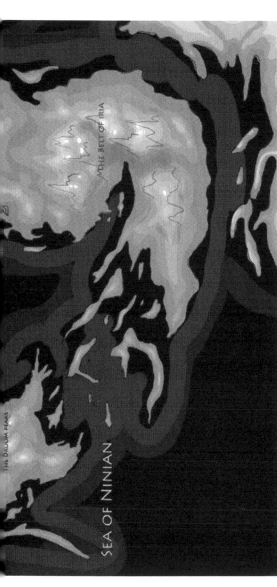

SEA OF NINIAN

THE BELT OF IRIA

THE DRUM PEAKS

THE WESTERN ISLES

- THE REFUGE
- THE RINGING BAY
- THE FEN
- TRABAILE
- ST AYRWYUS PRIORY
- TERMONDON
- DAWNS ABBEY
- THE VAIL OF NAOMHIN
- RIVER WYTHE

WEST FUNDLAND

- THE CAPITAL
- THE GREAT BAY
- BATTLEFIELD
- LIMESTONE QUARRY
- FARM
- THE FORGOTTEN RIVER
- GULLSWATER
- THE DEMESNE OF THE COPPER BEECHES
- SEASCALE

ACKNOWLEDGMENTS

Psalm 51:16-17 is from The Living Bible copyright © 1971. Used by permission of Tyndale House Publishers, Inc., Carol Stream, Illinois 60188. All rights reserved.

Shakespeare, William. "Literature Network – William Shakespeare – King Lear – Act 5. Scene III." *The Literature Network*. Jalic Inc., 2000-2016. Web. 12 Mar. 2016. http://www.online-literature.com /Shake speare/kinglear/27/

Spenser, Edmund. "Edmund Spenser - The Faerie Queene - Canto I." The Literature Network. Jalic Inc., 2000-2016. Web. 12 Mar. 2016. http://www.online-literature.com/edmund-spenser/faerie-queene/2/

A debt of thanks to Dawn and Steven R. Porter, Stillwater River Publications, for their help and expertise in making this print-on-demand novel possible.

Without Hollis Machala's visual expertise, her creative genius, and kind patience with me in helping develop the exterior and interior formatting of *the Penitent*, this story would still be in manuscript form. A deep debt of thanks goes to her for her invaluable assistance in helping make an idea be beautifully visible.

Jamie Forgetta is a freelance illustrator, author, and designer who worked with me for the first six months of 2019. She designed the three maps used in this trilogy. Many thanks to her for her superbly crafted visual work. Her patience is amazing and her ability to collaborate effectively with an author having no visual talent whatsoever is a miracle in itself. The quality of her work speaks for itself. She helped inspire some of the names of streets in the Seascale map and helped in getting some of the mountain ranges named for the main map depicting the setting of *the Penitent*. Her website is www.jamieforgetta.wixsite.com/portfolio

A profound debt of thanks goes to Carolyn for her support of this story, and for her helping edit the first draft: equally so to Kellie Kilgore and Susan Caspi for their editing help, and for their invaluable encouragement in my continuing to develop this story.

The map of St. Åyrwyus Priory that has been created here in this novel is based upon the first floor plan of the Fountains Cistercian Abbey, which is located near Aldfield, North Yorkshire, England. The image was found in Wikipedia at the following link https://en.wikipedia.org/wiki/Fountains_Abbey>. This image is in the public domain. The attribution states, "[English] A plan of Fountains Abbey taken from an early 20th century encyclo-pedia." The date of the image's first entry in Wikipedia is 6 February 2012.

I have seen the day, with my good biting falchion
I would have made them skip...

— William Shakespeare (1564–1616),
King Lear (1608)
— Act V, Scene iii, ll. 276 & 277

Led with delight, they thus beguile the way,
Vntill the blustering storme is ouerblowne;
When weening to returne, whence they did stray,
They cannot finde that path, which first was showne,
But wander too and fro in ways vnknowne,
Furthest from end then, when they nearest weene,
That makes them doubt, their wits be not their owne:
So many paths, so many turnings seene,
That which of them to take, in diuerse doubt they been.

— Edmund Spenser (1552–1599), *The Faerie Qveene* (1590)
— The First Book of The Faerie Qveene *Contayning*
— The Legende of the Knight of the Red Crosse, *or* of Holinesse
—Canto I, Stanza X

[16] You don't want penance;[a] if you did, how gladly I would do it! You aren't interested in offerings burned before you on the altar. [17] It is a broken spirit you want—remorse and penitence. A broken and contrite heart, O God, you will not ignore.

— Psalm 51:16 & 17 (*The Living Bible*)

Footnotes:
[a]Psalm 51:16 *penance*, literally "a sacrifice"

PROLOGUE | PROPOSITIONS SIX*

The singularity that is inevitably *coming will be man and Lucifer's chance to carve out a place; if not yet above, but alongside, the Creator's. Mankind will truly learn what it means to <u>dis</u>assemble. The rest of us will be brought into this <u>dys</u>topic[40] montage[41] of evil playing itself out presently on the world canvas in a vast sense of dis*ease. *It will be a contagion of mind and a pandemic of conscience fluorescing into all levels of humanity's values at greater and exponentially increasing rates. There will be an avalanche of deceit in which people will earnestly embrace as the truth.*

An intelligent person considers *possibilities; an educated one objectively examines ideas and entertains those that are opposite of his or her own predilections.[42] Nevertheless, this scenario that engages us so fiercely now, is one in which a wise person prepares for the worst while hoping for the best. This wise individual selects a strategy, picks a perspective, and makes a conceptual choice dance into practice, especially in order to save the lives of the people s/he loves.*

If we but listen figuratively to such wisdom, we could at least consider my statement here as a thought experiment—an ideational exercise. Affectively, I am sure that it translates well into a trenchant cry in at least three of the world's three great Abrahamic religions: "Gird your loins with the full armor of God.[246] The angels will trumpet[247] in Armageddon.[248] The seals will be opened.[249] The vials will be poured out[250]: The Four Horsemen[251] will canter forth an Apocalypse[252] unto the world's attention."

These occurrences are ancient in their determination to happen. They are inexorable in their proleptic[156] demand for such reality to blossom into our own time, and their very need to unfold into a preordained, historical manifestation only indicates impatient hesitation on their behalf, as well as the momentum guiding them; yet, they will but presently ensue in full force.

Such causes await their attendant effects; they have to proceed because all the forces and omens[51] are assembling into play for them to ignite into being, into an outpouring that includes mythology, legend and wisdom equally being awakened. Thus, today I await for the Cumaean sibyl[016] to offer her insight into the future; I anticipate a fifteenth book of the Sibylline Oracles[017] to be newly found and read to mankind; and, I pray that I live to hear the voices of a Daniel and a Matthew, a thaumaturge, a nabi or a Tay al-Ard speak aloud of it to me.

I envy Simeon who in his old *age still tarried on Earth, within the holy temple of ancient Jerusalem, waiting for the consolation of Israel.[14-15]*

-Professor Melvin Tobin, Ph.D.
-Cambridge, Massachusetts, Old Earth

*Statement first excerpted from a retirement speech, "U†opia Imperiled," given by Dr. Tobin at the Harvard Club.

*Tobin, M. (2156, July 15). †The philosophical primacy[1] of intelligence engineering[2] permeating throughout advanced evolutionary intervention.**56** The Journal of Ideation & Consilience,* **H**ologram **C**odex 18: 2287.299 | 12 – **NASCENT: 2057-2058**. *Retrieved Epicycle 07, 2252*

CHAPTER ONE

She had been in this small house in the woods ever since she could remember being there. It was home to her, even though it was not her first one. While it was a simple and humble dwelling, everything in it was comfortable to her, and thoughtfully placed just in the right spots.

She did not live with her parents. She had been adopted informally by Matthew Greatworth. Matthew called himself a hermit. However, folks who lived nearby considered him merely a recluse. In any event, hermit, recluse, both, or none at all, Matthew withdrew himself from the company of humans because he felt distracted by them. Alone, without the ongoing trauma and drama of living amongst mortals, Matthew could seek the living presence of God.

He was free from the daily chores of social and community obligations. When he felt the hand of God upon him, he could investigate, pray and discern this touch of the divine will with as much concentration as he cared to expend on it. No one bothered him. He bothered no one at all. Matthew would sometimes characterize these two former statements as having great worth.

"And, that's why the good God gave me my name," he would chuckle.

While he was very practical, he was also very absentminded, particularly when he was communing in the spirit.

It was Matthew who found her.

She had been but a baby abandoned by fate, human cruelty, or the lord of sin on a rural road. Greatworth would argue with himself over this very issue for many years. Her parents were lying dead in the middle of the lane. Their throats cut. Their bodies violated. There was no mercy to be had in this scene. Except for the fact that an intuition of danger crossed her mother's awareness before she and her husband were so senselessly murdered, Jacquelyn Blessingvale would never be thinking the thoughts pouring out of her memories even now. She would have been dead.

That day of prophetic mercy saw one of the many roving bands of outlaws in the Western Isles raiding the Blessingvale caravan.

Her mother's intuition and foresight spared her baby's life. Before these brigands brutalized the Blessingvales, she had run unobserved off the road. She carried her child to a ditch and placed her in the bottom. A thicket of alders next to it helped camouflage the spot even more. The baby was swaddled securely and covered with a blanket.

Less than a day after this fatal tragedy occurred, Matthew was in one of his distracted phases. He was not paying attention to where he was walking. As a matter of fact, he was off to the side of the road, strolling along in a roughly parallel position with it. He was arguing with himself over some arcane matter concerning the nature of a miracle.

The laws of nature are suspended when a miracle occurs, was one of the strands of argument he was considering.

"Although," he countered aloud to no one in particular, "the very fact that a miracle occurs may mean that the laws of nature aren't suspended, but fulfilled instead."

Well, if that is true, miracles should be occurring all of the time, but they don't.

"Matthew, just because one cannot see such with the eyes of man, does not mean that miracles are not occurring."

True, true, but this is mere confusion. When a blind man's sight is healed with the touch of a prophet, the laws of sickness, maladies and death are set aside. If these axioms were not set aside there would be no miracle.

"Look here, a miracle happens because the presence of God is the realization of natural and spiritual law. Every moment in time is filled with this potential. We have but to invoke it in faith for it to be seen in our presence. It's like falling..."

With the last statement being uttered, Matthew, not looking at all where he was going, fell into what looked like an old trench. When he hit the bottom of it, he completed his proposition saying, "...into a ditch."

Finding himself lying on his back at the bottom, he stared uncomprehendingly at the sky above him. Gaining his wits about him, he railed at himself internally, *What kind of miracle is this now*?

Matthew stood up and shook the dirt and dust off him. He looked to see if he was still hale. He checked for cuts, bruises or sprains.

Seeing that he was just fine he said, "No broken bones: looks like a minor miracle just occurred."

The hermit moved to his right to get a better purchase onto the ground so he could work his way out of the somewhat deep furrow into which he had fallen. He felt his foot hit something soft. Paying no attention to it, he concentrated on getting out of the ditch.

He reached the top and started walking away.

He thought he mistakenly heard the faint snuffle and low gurgling of a baby.

Of late, he had been hearing many odd noises. He passed it off as an internal clangor and mental noise that comes with being an older person.

"Perhaps these sounds I am hearing are just a result of my infernal caterwauling to myself," he said with a distracted and impatient air.

I am just going to let two auditory hallucinations of a baby rattle away somewhere else, he added to himself internally with growing irritation.

Assured with the fact that he had solved this annoyance to his satisfaction, Greatworth continued walking. "Thank the good Lord; I'm out of that trap to the unwary."

Mere misapprehension, Matthew snorted derisively. *I may as well think I heard a troll tell me a new perspective on the origins of life where I fell.*

"It could well be an angel," he countered.

Or, a very clever troll, came his immediate response.

Behind him, a baby's laughing and cooing resounded from the side of the road into which he had tumbled.

Both sides of him, now curious to discover the true origin of these sounds, became quiet and ceased their argument with one another. He took what he appeared to be hearing as a sign to go back over to the ditch and investigate further. He used the baby's voice as a beacon to guide himself by and soon found her lying near the bottom of the trench from which he had just extracted himself.

Picking her up carefully, and cooing to her, in turn, as he carried her back out of the ditch, he reached level ground. Matthew sat down on the side of the road with her still in his arms.

After a while, the misshapen bodies, broken and pillaged cart in the center of the road, and scattered and ripped clothes of the miserable tableau before him, attracted his attention. He got up onto his feet and looked around at an appalling scene of pillage and rapine.

Upon looking closer at the details of this crime, he found a leather pouch thrown carelessly on top of a small opened case. He set both aside for his purposes of rescuing her from this scene. With one hand holding the baby, he used the other to gather together any of her clothing he could find into the case. Any papers that he also found were put into the leather pouch. There were no valuables, coin or jewelry, in evidence.

He completed his task of collecting the items he thought a baby would need.

Looking over all of the carnage committed there, while keeping the babe in his gentle but firm grasp, he prayed over the dead.

When he was finished praying, he looked at the baby again. She looked back at him with a steadiness and intelligence that melted his old heart.

"How did you survive this attack, little one?" he gently asked her.

Someone, her mother or father, must have put her in the trench for safekeeping, he considered silently.

"These bodies have been here awhile: at least a day. It's a miracle she's survived this violence, and another one as well that she's not dead from starvation, thirst or the further depredation of humans and wild animals."

Looks like we have found an angel after all, he wryly said to himself. *There is goodness and innocence in the world if we but look for it.*

"Yes," he agreed. "Good news has always been told by the angels of the Lord."

I think we should name her... he said silently. "Evangel," he completed aloud.

CHAPTER TWO

Matthew had taken her to his forest home. He called the forest God's Temple. The home he lived in was called The Refuge.

When the weather was warm, both of them would bring into their household flowers, leaves and anything interesting that they could easily carry with them. These daily trophies of nature's beauty were used to great effect in decorating the small home.

"It isn't much," she frequently said aloud to the house, "but it's perfect, nevertheless."

Indeed, he had the time to build himself a very comfortable hermitage.

The Refuge had a common room, which Matthew called "a great room". In this area was a fireplace that served the purposes of providing heat, light and a place to cook food. A medium sized, oaken table, built with his own hands, sat near a window where they ate their meals. A small, compact room was used as a library and devotional for Matthew. Matthew slept in the bedroom on the first floor. Evangel used the loft for her sleeping quarters. There was a cupboard area for storing seasonings, spices and herbs, as well as for holding utensils used for cooking and eating. A larger pantry–like space was set aside for the making and keeping of bread, including the food preparation for meals. It also served as a dry larder of sorts containing different kinds of hard-rind cheeses, grains, cereals, dried fruits and nuts. A limited amount of space was also used for ale, brandy and wine that Matthew obtained from St. Åyrwyus Priory and Dawn's Abbey.

A basement underneath the floor of the great room was used as a wet larder. Not only were meats and game kept there, but it also held uncooked meat and vegetables.

All in all, it was a place of comfort; a true home in the wilderness.

Long ago, when Matthew first found this spot, he built a temporary structure to live in nearby while he built his home. When he was finished constructing it, he knocked down the makeshift quarters and put in its place a hidden safe room underneath the ground. He never had to use it, but he believed in providing contingencies against "any random events, and purposeful attacks, from hell, or from human beings, and even bad weather, for that matter."

A case in point is what happened to Evangel's parents, he would sometimes emphasize to himself.

Matthew never seemed at a loss to help her adjust to the different phases of her growing up. He would tell her in his own unique way what life was offering, or denying, her. And she understood what he was trying to say to her.

Despite his care, and probably because of it, in making sure that she had a good description of her parents and who they were to her, she loved Matthew as if he were the grandfather the Good Lord gave her on this worldly plane.

As she became older and the issues of life became more complex, Matthew was able to explain to her in a more mature way the complexity about what was happening inside her. If he could not help her, he would find a way to do so. For example, when she first became a woman he brought one of the nuns from the not too distant St. Åyrwyus Priory to stay with them for a month. Her name was Murial. The two women became close friends with one another.

In taking care of Evangel, Matthew was always careful to tell her who her parents were. Even though he had never met them, he knew enough about them from what he could glean from other people who had known them. He had also read a diary that both her father and mother kept. He also thought it important that their memory be kept sacred and honored for her.

Matthew told her early on in the young girl's life that her surname was Blessingvale. "Your first name was Jacquelyn."

"Isn't that my name still?" she would ask him.

"Yes, child," he responded. "But the name God gave you through me is Evangel."

"Can I still keep my last name, Grandfather?"

Matthew nodded distractedly at her as he was already becoming lost in an internal argument with himself over the corruption of holy vows in the Church.

"Evangel Blessingvale," she pronounced slowly and with pride. "Sounds like a holy prophet, doesn't it, Grandfather?"

"Mmmmmnnn, more like prophetess, lass."

"Does a prophetess get to talk with God almost every day, too?" She first asked him this question when she was very young. It was often one—as was the topic of this conversation—that became almost a ritual of discussion between them.

Her comment helped bring Greatworth back in the moment, especially in paying greater attention to her and what she was conveying to him. "I think that goes with the crops in the fields, as with the trees in the forest, and the fish in the sea, little one."

11

"You always answer me with funny words."

"Yes, Evangel," he replied with a slight hint of exasperation. "A prophetess is a girl, or a woman, who does talk with God almost every day. Please forgive my inattention."

"It's okay, Grandfather, I know you're trying to talk with yourself about something important."

Matthew smiled at the generosity of spirit she always showed him.

He was never mad with her. While she was a child who was full of life, energy and the restlessness of curiosity, he never had reason to become upset with her over bad behavior. A part of him wanted her to adopt his last name because she profoundly had become a great worth to him.

Evangel Greatworth sounds exactly right to me, he mused with certitude.

A thought tugged on him concerning what she had just asked him about being with God. "Does God talk with you?" he asked.

"No, Grandfather, I talk with him mostly."

"Mostly!" he said somewhat surprised.

She looked at him with her hazel green eyes and nodded her head in agreement.

"Does God answer you sometimes, child?" he asked with gentle and great interest.

Again, she looked at him and nodded her head.

"Do you hear His voice," he asked in awe.

12

"No," she answered right away. "He sometimes shows me things, though."

Greatworth now said nothing. He looked at the little girl before him with a childlike simplicity of his own. He waited patiently for her to explain more about what she had just told him.

"He shows me in dreams, or in pictures. Sometimes a story comes to me and it's like you're reading it to me in a great book."

"What does the book look like?"

"It's on a table that's all alight and ringing like the bell at the priory. The book is in the middle of it. There are a lot of silver colored beings around in back of it. They're singing while holding glowing spears in their hands."

Matthew blinked his eyes rapidly on hearing this information. "And, the book...."

"The book is hard to see because it keeps changing. The light pouring from it is brighter than the sun's."

"How do you know what's in it, dear one?"

"I hear your voice reading from it, Grandfather."

While Matthew had many other questions he wanted to ask her, he held off in doing so. She had just given him enough information for him to consider for a season, and then some.

When she was eleven years of age, she went on a walk to one of her favorite places in the woods. It was a place that she had not visited for a while since the early spring. Thus, she was anxious to get there and see what nature had done in the meantime to it.

The pool of water with fish swimming in its depths was the same as it was the last time she was there. If anything, the depth of the water was a bit lower. The stream had not been replenished by the blessing of rain for almost a month. The amount of water flowing over a series of waterfalls leading to it had significantly been lowered, too. The sound of it cascading over the rocks was not as loud as it had been when she was there last.

"Well, that simply makes it better for me to *hear* what else is happening *here*," she said audibly just to listen to the rhyme and the play on the same sounding words she made up on the spot.

She sat down near the pool's edge and leaned her head back against a young tree. The leaves in the oak tree above her rustled slowly in the gentle wind's caress. The stream pouring into the pool below her conversed with the leaves overhead in watery chattiness.

She fell asleep.

On the other side of the pool, deeper into the woods, a young wolf was giving birth to her first litter. It was struggling to stay alive in bringing her pups into the world.

Evangel could see this event happening in her dream. She could sense there was something different about this animal. Several powers had settled on it. Three distinct entities coalesced their might into its pain-wracked body.

She felt no ill will in this triune force. She felt love, loyalty and a lethal desire to seek a wrong righted within it. She could not identify the source of this wrong.

Seven pups were delivered. Only three survived. They were very small. In truth, they were tiny. They were pure white. In the succession of their being birthed, one whined plaintively, the other gave a soft, husky sigh, while the third gasped, coughed and gulped for air desperately.

Arising from the dream, she unerringly went to the place where the mother wolf had given birth. When she arrived there, she found the wolf dead.

Tears fell from her eyes.

"Just like me," she said. "Born into the world with death all around you. No mother and father to protect you."

15

Don't be such a foolish goose, she thought to herself. *These are just animals.*

"They may be on the surface, but God showed me they are from his will."

She realized with a shock that she was talking to herself the way Matthew often did as well.

She became further surprised when she saw that she had come across a scene of tragedy just like her grandfather had so long ago when he found her in a ditch alongside the road.

"Well, there's nothing else to do but to take these three living ones home for Grandfather and I to take care of them."

What will you name them? she asked herself.

"Why that's simple. God's spirit already told me: Whimper, Whisper and Wheezer."

She carried them home with her.

When she told Matthew the story, he knelt down and hugged her. As tears fell from his eyes, he said, "Just like you said to yourself, you were brought to them by the Lord above to save and care for them. Like grandfather, like granddaughter."

Both laughed through their tears.

Matthew had Evangel bring him to the scene of the puppies' birth. He had brought a shovel with him. "We need to bury their mother and the other pups properly, and send them along with grace and mercy back to the Lord's domain."

With loving care all five animals were buried, and blessed as well with prayer and song.

They returned home soon afterwards.

When they arrived at the door to The Refuge, Evangel looked up at Matthew and asked, "Does this mean that I am to be their grandmother, Matthew?"

Her use of his first name startled him. "No, child," he responded solemnly, "I would say that you are now a prophetess and protector to them."

———————

Six years passed in the peace and in the prosperity of Matthew's profound care for her and for their three wards.

The time, on gossamer wings undaunted in its rush towards destiny, carried them in its swift current.

Life for these five was idyllic. This sylvan span of time since Greatworth found her, stretching in length for almost a score of years, was shattered in her seventeenth.

CHAPTER THREE

On an evening in midwinter, Evangel and Matthew were preparing to retire for the night. It had been unseasonably cold. The snow lay deep on the land. Travel between The Refuge and the nearby monastery and priory was halted. No one could get through to one another because of the severe and adverse weather they had been experiencing for the last six weeks.

Matthew finished up his reading and meditations in his library.

Evangel cleaned and put everything away. She banked the fire in the fireplace and made sure that there was plenty of wood nearby the hearth to keep it going throughout the night.

Matthew went around to the door and windows, making sure they were tightly closed. He checked to see there were no gaps anywhere to keep the gelid air from invading into their home.

Whimper and Whisper moved to their places for the night, curling up in front of the fire screen set before the hearth. Matthew had made low lying cots for them to relax or sleep on, but they rarely used them. The three wolves were still very small for their kind. Indeed, they did not look very wolflike at all. Whisper was the heaviest one and weighed fifteen pounds. Whimper was about ten pounds in weight.

Evangel carried Wheezer, who was all of seven pounds, up the loft ladder where she placed him on her bed. Of the three wolves, he loved her the most. While all three wolves and two humans were inseparable from one another, Wheezer was like Evangel's alter ego. If he could he would be underfoot, or hopping on all four paws in front of her, hoping that she would pick him up and carry him around with her. Often, she did take "pity" on him. She would scoop him up in her arms and carry the petite white wolf around the house. She developed a little carrier for him that went around her neck. She would often take him with her on walks and carry him in her sling while the other two wolves followed closely beside her.

Once on the bed, he would brush himself up against the pillow, sneeze several times and pant happily from his nighttime ritual of getting ready to sleep. When she got under the covers and rested on her back, he would snuggle up against her left shoulder. The miniature sized wolf would remain on top of the bedclothes most of the night. Just before dawn, he would get over on the other side of the bed— *the outside edge, or the one away from the wall*—and sleep next to her head. If she slept on her side, though, he would curl up against the small of her back.

19

Her nickname for him was "B", which didn't make much sense to her because it had nothing to do with the name given him by her. She knew that it just felt right calling him that sometimes.

"You know, B," she often would tell him, "you're a real pest. You just want to be warm."

He would just look at her while keeping his head between his front paws.

"I think you're laughing at me!"

Wheezer would close his eyes and look like he had fallen asleep.

"Come now, Wheezer, you can't have gone to sleep so fast."

The wolf would open one eye and thump his small white tail against the blanket.

Evangel would laugh aloud heartily, and then talk with him about the day's events. When she was done sharing with him her thoughts about them, she would say her prayers. For some reason, especially if she had forgotten to pray for someone or something, the wolf would keep his eyes open. After addressing any omission in her petition, she would see if everything was now okay for her to sleep. If it was, his eyes were closed.

She said her prayers and when she finished doing so, she checked to see if the wolf's eyes were open or closed.

They were open.

She continued with her prayers and came to a stop. She looked over at the wolf:

His eyes were still open.

This same routine went on for a bit longer.

Finally, in sheer frustration with him, she exclaimed, "All right, you're being impossible. I think you're asleep with your eyes open. Or, are you playing a trick on me? Which is it B? Get it out. What am I missing?"

The wolf just stared at her.

"Okay, you are now starting to get me worried."

The wolf continued to stare at her, this time without blinking.

"You know I should try that trick with Grandfather and see how far it would get me in not blinking my eyes."

The wolf raised his head off his paws and looked up at the ceiling above them.

"Lord," she said in exasperation, "this tiny wolf that you have given me is something I thank you for from the bottom of my heart." She closed her eyes at this point and continued with her prayer. "I ask that you protect all of us in this dear home: that your angels place a hedge around it and our mortal souls. I ask for a mighty blessing on us and that this terrible cold and snow soon be gone. Amen."

21

She looked over at the wolf.

Wheezer's eyes were closed. He was snoring.

Evangel shook her head and laughed quietly.

Soon, she was asleep and lightly snoring along with the small wolf by her side.

In the dawn's rose-colored light they arose.

Other than greeting Matthew with a distracted, "Good morning, Grandfather," Evangel said nothing else to him. She was not exactly out of sorts, but preoccupied about something else concerning her.

Observing her closely, Matthew realized that she was having a debate because she was talking quietly to herself, sometimes in a heated whisper. *I should recognize the signs of an internal meditational debate. I certainly have enough of them.*

"Child, are you well this early morning?" he asked her when they were sitting down to the table breaking their fast.

"I don't know, Grandfather," she said after hesitating how best to answer his question.

"What is disturbing you, then?"

"I had a strange but amazing dream last night."

"Pray thee, young one, may I hear what it was about."

She nodded her head in affirmation to his request, but then remained silent for a while.

Not being able to wait for her answer any longer, Matthew again asked, "What is it that is vexing you?"

Again, she remained quiet for a bit. She raised her eyes and looked at him saying, "I had a strange dream last night, Grandfather."

"I know, dear one, you told me thus," he patiently said.

Without providing a context or setting for the dream, she said, "There was a man who walked out of the rule of law."

The hairs on the back of Matthew's neck rose. He stopped eating and pushed his bowl away from him. "Yes...." was the only word he could muster aloud.

She nodded her head in a silent confirmation with his one word utterance. "He was a carpenter. I saw soldiers nail him to wood."

Mathew turned pale. She was stating something he knew to be deeply true. But what she was saying, had certain authorities heard it as well, would be considered decidedly heretical. She could be burned at the stake for such words.

All three wolves came near her and sat down on their haunches between the two humans.

They curiously wanted to be a part of this conversation.

"Yes, Evangel, go on. Tell me more about the dream."

"He was on a cross and arose from it," she said in wonder.

"He fulfilled the price of our death with his blood," Matthew acknowledged.

She nodded in agreement to his statement.

"Nothing in our books tells us this, child," he said softly.

"Yes," she said, and paused. "But it's in the one that counts."

"You mean the one on the table where the angels are singing and holding their spears that are glowing?"

"Yes. He walked on a different world than ours and said that he would set the captives free. What does that mean, Grandfather?"

"About what He said or that you saw Him on a different world?" he responded.

"Both, I guess. I never thought of anything like this. But when I saw him I knew it was true. When he was hanging there, he looked straight into my eyes and smiled."

Matthew remained quiet.

"When he smiled at me, he was no longer on this awful tree. We were walking on a beautiful road. He showed me many things. We went and talked together underneath the shade of a wood filled with copper beech trees and a stream flowing in the middle of them."

"This is as it should be, Evangel."

"Why do you tell me this, Grandfather?"

"Because you are blessed, first, with the good news. And second, this was given to you in fulfillment of his sacrifice. Third, it is a commission for you to fulfill the name given you on the road where your parents were slain."

"Have you seen this one as I have?" she asked.

"I have felt His presence in my heart since I was a child," he responded.

"Have you spoken with him? Did you tell others?" she queried in quick succession.

He paused to consider her questions. "I speak with Him all of the time, but I have never heard Him aloud. I have not told anyone else about these things except with you on this morn."

"Why not?"

"The clerics who are alive today do not believe in Him. It is death to speak of such matters to them, or to others."

The young woman and the old man became silent. Both were deep in thought.

Matthew arose from the table and went over to the door to open it. Thick ice had formed

25

overnight, particularly on its outer edges of the frame. Once he managed to pull the inner door free towards him, he had to knock off the ice on the outer one as well before pushing it open away from him. Upon doing so, he glimpsed outside quickly. Soft, fat flakes of snow were falling rapidly to the ground.

After securing both doors once more, he walked back to the table and put his hand on one of her shoulders. "We need to start the day, child. It looks like we have another snowfall to bear."

"But, Grandfather, I saw other things, too," she said hesitantly.

Greatworth sighed not with frustration, but with concern over what else she was going to tell him. "Can you share them with me, Evangel?" he asked as he sat back down in his chair.

Again without offering a prologue to answering his question, she replied, "We are being watched."

Greatworth held his breath. *Here it announces itself as I have dreamed it would*, he thought.

"The Lord helped me see that we are being watched from a place that is both distant from us, yet it as if they are right here in this very room watching us."

"How are they both far away and close to us at the same time?" He asked her.

"They are beings who are far beyond our ken. They have a dread hunger for greater knowledge. Their desire for power is without limits."

"Are they evil?"

"I think they are playing with us and they serve their own ends."

Matthew was just as much stunned at the elegant simplicity of her answer as well as being speechless over its implication.

They remained quiet for a while.

The three wolves looked at one another and howled.

The fire popped in its hunger to spill warmth into the room.

The sap in the trees outside snapped in mutual report with the sparks going off in The Refuge's hearth.

For many days afterward, Matthew pondered these things in his heart.

CHAPTER FOUR

The fierce cold gradually lessened. The winter released its hold onto the land.

Spring, beckoning from a distance for far too long over the winter months, now held forth with her merciful warmth and rain.

In the early morning of what would become a pleasant late April day, Evangel set out to meet Murial and Juliana, who was an oblate sister at St. Åyrwyus Priory. At least two or three times a year when weather and travel conditions allowed, the priory, or Dawn's Abbey, which was the monastery that was further up the road in the Vale of Naomhin, sent someone with supplies to Matthew. Murial had been making most of these trips since she had first met Evangel. As this meeting was a planned one, Evangel only had to walk half the distance to join up with them. This arrangement saved her having to walk the entire way, which normally would have taken her well over half a day to reach the holy order of women. The three wolves, as usual, accompanied the young woman. They started out overflowing with an abundance of energy. Jumping on one another, racing around in circles, wrestling and bounding off to investigate anything that deserved to be looked at, they were excited to start an adventure with her.

"You three need to save your strength," she scolded them with a laugh. "You'll be tired out in no time, and then how am I going to carry all three of you: answer me that now, will you!"

All three animals stopped and looked at her with their tongues hanging out, panting fiercely.

"Mmnnhumph, just as I said. Look at you. You're getting exhausted all ready. Maybe you should stay with Grandfather today, instead of going with me."

If wolves, especially small ones, could appear sheepish, these three certainly put on an excellent act in gazing diffidently at her.

"Oh, stop staring at me that way," she chided them once more. "You look downright foolish. You might even bleat at me."

Upon hearing her laugh once more, they sprang up onto all four paws and raced around her several times while she laughed merrily at their antics.

When they had gone over a mile, the wolves settled into a comfortable pace beside her. She hummed out loud to herself, talked to the wolves frequently and commented upon many of the beautiful sights they saw from the path they were following. The morning passed pleasantly by and when the sun was at its zenith, she stopped to rest briefly.

The innocence of the day, while it was beguiling to her, did not overly influence her outlook on her life; she still felt very out of sorts. Like Matthew, she carried on a conversation with herself. The wolves had dropped around her to the ground when she had stopped and were taking a nap.

"I know I am blessed by many things," she said aloud once she had settled in a seated position.

But I have been shown more than anyone can bear, she thought to herself.

"Yet, being shown what I've been given is a blessing as well."

The blessings are wondrous, indeed, but the burden of them is quite another matter.

Evangel sighed at this last internal statement. She remained quiet and intended only to close her eyes briefly to rest. She slept for about an hour.

She awoke because all three wolves were standing around her and growling at something down the trail towards The Refuge. She felt disquieted not only at their manner, but also over the fact that nothing tangible came to her from any of the images she knew she had just dreamed.

She could not recall anything from her sleep. It had been a disturbing one. Instead of feeling rested and refreshed from her break in walking, she felt tainted somehow by she knew not what.

Voices sounded in the distance, on the opposite side of her, on the path in the direction of the priory. When they came closer, she could tell they were women talking with one another, especially when they laughed. She recognized Muriel's laughter immediately as the sister had a distinctive sound of deep enjoyment when she thought something was humorous to her.

The young woman was embarrassed that she fell asleep. Getting her bearings more fully, she hastened down the path toward them.

Two of the wolves, getting the scent of the pair of women, bounded off ahead of her to greet Muriel and Juliana.

"As usual," she said to the one remaining with her, "my faithful Wheeze stays with me, huh, B?" she complimented him.

He looked up at her and wagged his tail.

"You know, I don't know if wolves wag their tails much, but you sure do." She bent down and picked him up in her arms. He snuggled closer into her.

She hurried to meet her company.

31

Muriel and Juliana had brought two mules with them. These animals were heavily laden and packed with not only necessary items belonging to the two women, but also with supplies and foodstuffs for The Refuge. Each woman was holding a mule by the halter grimly when Evangel came running down the path to greet them shyly.

Whimper and Whisper were racing around them with joy and unreserved energy.

The mules did not appreciate this zestful reception. Both balked at the two, four-legged sprites running around and underneath them. First one, then the other mule started braying.

"Pray you, forgive me for not meeting you at our assigned place. I took a rest from my walk," she said to them breathlessly while sweeping the two wolves that had run on ahead back to her side.

Attempting to shake her head in dismay, Muriel mostly held onto her fractious mule. She was trying to prevent it from bolting away from her and running back down the trail toward the priory. She looked quickly over to her oblate sister and noted that she was experiencing the same difficulty in tending to her mule.

Evangel started laughing. The two wolves near her sat down and gave short, rapid barks.

Wheezer wagged his tail frenetically and sat up in her arms.

The two sisters at first seemed insulted at this response. Seeing the joy of love and friendship pouring out of Evangel toward them so effusively, they let go of the mules and started laughing heartily as well.

The mules, in turn, felt the pressure on their halters completely go slack and free. They raised their heads in surprise and prepared themselves to run away. However, the laughter and total lack of concern about what they were about to do puzzled them. Instead of scattering away, they stayed in place. Initially reluctant to do so, they became docile and then snorted out their delight at stopping.

The three women greeted one another. Evangel made a fuss over the mules. Muriel and Juliana greeted the three wolves, praised them and gave each of them a small piece of jerky.

Juliana took pity on Whimper and Whisper saying to them with mock pretension, "Certainly, your journey to reach us on this perilous road has been an arduous one. Would your lords like to ride on our loyal coursers here and rest your weary paws from the strife of your labors?"

For some reason, her words had a chilling effect on Evangel. The gaiety she felt a moment ago drained away from her immediately.

Seeing her mood swing so dramatically from mirth to misgiving, Juliana asked her, "Are you alright, child? What harm have my words to these wonderful wolves caused you?"

Muriel went over to her and held one of Evangel's hands.

"Your words, while innocently given, and in fondness for me and mine, have caused a fey feeling to overwhelm me."

The two older women said nothing regarding her comment. They waited to hear what more she would say to help explain the somber shift in her mood.

"I am late in meeting you because in taking a brief respite from walking on this path to join up with you, I fell asleep without meaning to."

Juliana joined Muriel, and held Evangel's other hand in worried compassion over her friend's consternation.

"I dreamt about The Refuge. There was something...bad happening...." She paused in trying to describe her vision. "These three," indicating the wolves around them, for even Wheezer had jumped out of her arms to join his brothers in celebrating their meeting Evangel's friends, "were very upset. "They became..."

She stopped explaining suddenly and acted as though she was listening to something far away

34

or very muted in volume and was straining to hear it correctly.

"We must hurry back to The Refuge in the greatest haste we can summon," she pronounced.

The three wolves had come close to her. Muriel said, "They seem to agree with you. But something else seems to concern them, too."

"Yes, Muriel, but we must hasten onwards now. Kindly put the small ones on the mules," she said as she turned back towards her home in the woods. "Grandfather is in trouble."

The trip back to The Refuge remained a blur to Evangel. She was, at first, filled with anxiety and fear over the fate of her grandfather. She battled these feelings as though she were physically dealing with avowed enemies whose sole purpose was to overthrow her sense of comfort and peace. She began praying for help to the one she had dreamed about and whose presence she announced to Matthew.

At one point in their return to her home, she told Muriel and Juliana the dream she had the night before and the fate of the carpenter she was shown in her sleep.

This news filled both women with concern over Evangel's sanity and safety. Their orders, along with the rest of the clerical and monastic worlds, did not share such a vision at all, especially as in the

35

one the young woman hurriedly communed with them.

Within three miles of reaching her home, the wolves became restless. They started growling. The hair on the scruff of their necks stood up as though they were reacting to an actual threat standing directly in front of them. Whimper, then Whisper, tried to jump off the mule on which each one was riding.

"Let all three off the mules," Evangel gently ordered.

With great alacrity, Juliana lifted them out of the carriers they were so anxiously trying to get out of, and placed them on the ground.

Upon being put there, they raced off as one towards Evangel's home.

"I've never seen them act so," she worriedly admitted.

After watching the wolves disappear from their sight, all three women quickly proceeded down the path.

When they were about half a mile from The Refuge, Muriel cautioned them saying, "If, indeed, Evangel's fears and the wolves' unrest are correct, and I am afraid they are just to be so concerned, we must be cautious how we approach the hermit's refuge."

Juliana agreed with her superior, "Yes, Muriel, we also need to put up the mules here securely and not have any encumbrance from them in seeking out what may have happened or befallen Matthew."

"I know a way of getting there from here," Evangel informed them. "There is a slight path in the wood we can take that will bring us to the back of the house where Matthew splits wood for our hearth."

"Yes, child," agreed Muriel, "take us that way. We are here beside you."

"Once there, daughter, can we look upon the home unobserved, yet with discernment about what may be happening around The Refuge?" asked Juliana.

"Yes," Evangel simply declared.

The mules' burdens were taken off of them and placed safely aside out of their reach. Free of their cumbersome packs, they were now firmly tied in a picket hobble. A small collar like device was put onto only one front leg of each mule. The mules seemed comfortable with the hobbles being fastened just above the fetlock, on the cannon bone itself, above the hoof of the animals and just below the knee. They were also tied off between two trees by a rope that was placed overhead them.

During the time this procedure was being completed by Muriel and Juliana, Evangel paced back and forth just out of reach of the ropes securing the mules.

Muriel checked their work to see that the hobbles were on just tightly enough and that they did not chafe or unduly hurt the animals. She had Juliana scrutinize the area where the mules would be stationed to see if there were any obstructions that might hurt the mules or entangle them in the rope to which they were tied. Satisfied that they were safe and secure, the women joined Evangel. They all worked their way through dense woods onto a very small path leading towards Matthew's home.

CHAPTER FIVE

It was when the women were within about five hundred yards to the house that they heard raised voices. The wind had been blowing in the opposite direction, making it difficult for them to hear anything coming from The Refuge. Upon getting closer to this sound, they heard taunts being uttered and rough laughter breaking out of the mouths of at least a dozen men.

Not having to cover the sound of their movement so vigilantly any longer, the two sisters followed Evangel at a solid run. She halted at a screen of thick spruce at the edge of the opening field where the house was built. The women had a clear, but protected, view of the back of the house, especially where Matthew cut and stored the billets used to heat the home and to cook with them as well.

The hermit was on his knees with his hands tied in back of him. He was faced toward the chopping block upon which he used to split the wood, all of which was stacked carefully nearby in a beehive shape. A rope tied off in a noose was drawn tightly around his neck. It was held on the other end by a boy of fifteen years.

Not including the boy, Muriel counted a total of fifteen men present in the small yard. Signaling to Juliana by hand the number she observed, Juliana nodded in agreement with her sister's tally.

Muriel also silently gestured Evangel to stay in place.

"Osbert Tabard's the name old man from whom you have the honor in being treated by with such courtesy," said a rough looking man standing over Matthew.

Men laughed without humor as they encircled the hermit.

"What is it you want from me, Master Tabard?" Matthew asked him.

"I don't believe I gave you leave to speak, hermit," Tabard countered. He gave a sideways nod of his head to the boy, who summarily jerked the rope roughly. Matthew fell onto his side.

"Ah," Tabard said without pity, "old age has its drawbacks, especially when a hempen rope pulled by a mere boy yanks you off your knees and plants your holy face into the dirt."

He let the old man stay in this awkward position.

Matthew coughed from the hideous pressure being brought to bear around his throat.

"What's that, recluse; I didn't catch what you said." More laughter and catcalls were voiced.

Tabard, feeling pleased with the state of affairs at the moment, said, "Seeing as you asked, anyways, what I, that is, what *we* all want from you is *your* money."

He signaled two other men to help get Matthew back onto his knees.

Murial again had to make sure that Evangel stayed still and remained quiet. She barely was able to restrain her from going to the rescue of her lifelong protector.

"Well, what do you have to say to that my old eremite?"

"I have no coin stored here, my son," Matthew hoarsely stated.

"Mmmmm," Tabard uttered. He stepped forward and backhanded the old man on the side of his head.

The boy jerked the rope again with the same result as before: Matthew fell face down onto the ground.

"Wrong answer, old one," Tabard said with disgust.

Men called out stark advice on what Tabard should do next.

"Get to the quick of the matter, your Honor and cut his manhood off," is a sample of what was being offered to Tabard.

"Let me state again," Tabard carefully enunciated, "Your money. It's due. We're here to collect it. Where is it?"

41

With his face still in the ground, Matthew said, "I have no wealth that rusts, such as you demand."

Tabard, with an expression of disdain on his face, went over to Matthew and kicked him in the precise spot in the head where he had just backhanded him with the palm of his hand.

He signaled his two helpers again to put the hermit back onto his knees in the same position and place as he had been in before he was wrenched onto the dirt.

While they were putting Matthew on his knees next to the chopping block, Tabard reached with his left hand over to the right side of his waist and drew a thinly shaped dagger from its sheath. "Well, old one, its lesson time. Hearken carefully to my words. This dagger is a type of rondel. It's stiff–bladed like my own personal poniard here often is," he pointed between his legs.

Laughter resounded throughout the yard. "Some rougher types call it—the knife, here in my hand—a yataghan or shashqa, depending on where they hail from."

He brought the hilt close to Matthew's eyes, explaining in a singsong lilt of his voice, "See, the pommel here looks like a human ear. That's why this little beauty is called an ear dagger. Any questions so far, my solitary ascetic?"

42

The old man feebly shook his head indicating he had none to ask his tormentor.

Tabard continued his instructional soliloquy about the weapon held in front of Matthew's face. "This particular handle is split in two. 'Why you ask?' It allows my thumb to be hooked on it, so I can give it a greater thrust against the object of my love," he obscenely added.

Whistles, catcalls and jeers spilled out from his band of men.

Their mockery bounded back and forth in the clearing in a clipped echo that shoved the women's sense of safety ever closer to perdition itself.

"I am losing my patience with you. Anyways, my instruction in words is about complete. The deed must be done that I intend to employ. The likes of 'Spinner' here, that's my love name for her, will not be used to assassinate you. I have something else in mind that serves a better purpose."

"So, share with me what I want to know before Spinner has to bite you, cenobite. Where is this treasure of 'great worth' everyone for leagues around here tells me you have?"

Matthew dolefully said, "My surname, as you have just employed it, was given as a holy designation only. The great treasure I have is not one found in this realm but lies within a man's heart and heaven's home."

Tabard sighed ruefully. "I am truly surfeited with your obdurate manner."

Putting his right hand on the back of Matthew's head, he brought the tip of Spinner's blade with his against the hermit's left eye. In one swift motion, he sunk the blade deftly into it and cut the orb out of its socket. Placing the old man's bloody eyeball on the block before him, he moved the blade quickly to Matthew's right eye.

The old man cried out in great distress.

"Not so full of yourself, are you now?" Tabard clinically observed.

Matthew breathed heavily and shook with fear. He whimpered in agonizing pain.

"Any time you want to tell me where your treasure is in the here and now, I'm eagerly waiting to hear it."

Blood ran down Matthew's face from the hollow cavity where his left eye had been.

Evangel shook off both women's pair of hands holding her in a vain attempt to keep her from leaping out into the circle, one where men avidly stood witnessing the degradation of the only person she loved and trusted.

Matthew was shaking violently. Three men now held him from whipping his head back and forth away from Spinner.

"What do you have to claim to me, solitary one?" Tabard pitilessly insisted.

"I have no claim on this world," the old man whispered.

Osbert Tabard tsked in disapproval at the hermit's last statement.

The outlaw cut out the hermit's right eye.

Wide applause to this cruel affliction broke out amongst the men surrounding him.

"Well, Matthew Noworth, you've put yourself in an even worse situation," Tabard announced. He placed the right eye in line next to the other one on the stump and faced their pupils derisively towards the old man.

Matthew, despite the grave insult done to him, and to the pain surging through him, held his head high. His blood slowed, but remained pulsing out of the orbit of his left eye in time with the beating of the hermit's heart. It still spilled freely from the other one.

"I know it is a dastardly thing I have done. But *look* at it this way. We've had our fun, such recompense that it is for our troubles. Yes, we're outlaws. Brigands. Thieves. Murderers... Undisciplined rabble of the worst sort. We're the Dread Rovers and I'm their dread leader."

Evangel stepped into the yard and quickly walked to the edge of the encircled men. Muriel and Juliana hurriedly followed her.

One of the rovers, espying the three women first, carnally grunted, "Ah, three scabbards to sheath our swords in."

Men parted to let them enter their circle, catcalling and moaning lecherously as the women walked by them.

Evangel, with Muriel and Juliana accompanying her closely, approached the leader of the Dread Rovers. Evangel demanded of him, "What great ill has made you wrought this rank work?"

"Why, Matthew," purred the outlaw, "you failed to mention that you have a stable of fine looking beauties here for you to play with. I can see why you're a holy man!"

Greatworth attempted to say something, but no words were stated. He turned his head towards the sound of Evangel's voice.

"I am sorely vexed at this shit!" Tabard roared. "Take these two older cows," pointing to Muriel and Juliana, and have sport with them in any way you like. Save this pearl for me. Stretch her out over there on the ground near her old man."

Again, under terrible duress and in great agony, Matthew attempted to say something, but failed in doing so.

Tabard looked at him closely. He patted the old man condescendingly on his head. "Okay, old one, you've earned the right to speak. I'll give you one chance to do so. Have your say...."

Matthew, in spite of the rope's pressure on his neck, as well as the three men holding him down on his knees, stood up on his feet. His eyes gored out, his face a wreck of blood, he boldly stood straight at attention.

After failing to speak audibly several times, he started coughing instead. In spite of the fit of wheezing he endured, everyone present clearly heard him say, "May the restoration of mercy rescue me."

Many of the men guffawed, chortled and laughed at the crazy old man. Some found Matthew's statement uncomfortable to hear. The boy holding the rope, whose noose was around the hermit's neck, dropped the rope as though it had been an adder spiting venom onto his face. He put his hand over his eyes as if he had gone blind instead of Matthew.

Three small shapes in a blur of white raced into the midst of the Dread Rovers.

CHAPTER SIX

Three diminutive wolves, racing like only the wind can on a stormy day, set themselves in place near Matthew and the three women. Men tried stomping on, or kicking at, them. Some with a quicker presence of mind tried swiping at them with their swords. Several knifes were thrown at the wolves, and two men decided that spitting in the wolves' general direction might dissuade them from being amongst them.

Regardless of the Rovers' futile attempts at controlling them, Whimper and Whisper moved alongside the hermit. Wheezer stopped at Evangel's side. All three animals looked at Matthew then at Tabard.

Tabard, regarding them with contempt and disdain said, more than asked, "What more pusillanimous bull's piss have you brought us Matthew, my misanthropic fool."

One Rover on the other side of the circle shouted, "Throw them three cutelins on a fire."

Another advised, "Can't eat em once their cooked cause there's nothin to em."

One of the men holding Greatworth said, "Ignore these three bootless bugbears. Finish the job on the old one. Have some entratainmint with these womin now."

"Matthew, do you see what you've caused me?" Tabard derisively asked. "I'm afraid I must move this farce along more hastily, don't you agree?" he added rhetorically.

Tabard shook his arms, stood on the balls of his feet, flexed the muscles in both arms and then ran in place briefly.

"Alright, men, hold the old trout still and I'll cut em up like a fresh caught fish."

Tabard drew Spinner back to strike a grievous blow on Matthew. The leader of the Rovers paused and said to the men standing around him, "Some of you lot take the older women and get going with them. Strip the pearl here down to her nubbins. I want her to watch the fun and see her get stirred up over my artistry here."

Men started moving to obey their leader's orders, not merely out of obedience, but from being eager to experience the potential pleasure that was to come.

The wolves were ignored. Muriel and Juliana were grabbed roughly and lewdly. Evangel was grabbed around the waist.

She raised her right arm back as soon as she was held. With her fist going over her left shoulder, the young woman twisted her torso to the left at the same time. She struck her elbow directly into the man's nose.

His eyes rolled up into the top of his head upon receiving this crushing strike. Blood gushed from his nose in a stream. His arms, becoming waxen, flopped by his sides. He fell to the ground dead.

Every Rover stopped at this seemingly impossible scene.

Silence held sway just for a moment.

Tabard started laughing. "Oh, I'm going to like moving with you, lass. You needs try that on me," he said to her while pointing at the dead Rover at her feet.

Stepping away from Greatworth, Tabard walked over to where Evangel was standing.

The adrenalin that was used in her self–defense made her shake as though she was sick with a virulent fever.

"Osbert!" One of the men called over to his leader.

Tabard chose to ignore him. Instead, he leaned into Evangel saying, "I'd take it as a privilege if you tried what you did to him with me."

"Osbert, you've got…" another voice sounded.

Tabard turned contemptuously with a sneer on his face to his men. "I don't 'got' to do anything but what I.…"

He was interrupted by something happening in the midst of them that he could not believe was possible.

The three small wolves, having been ignored after being pelted with verbal and physical abuse, were growing bigger. When Tabard finally turned his attention upon them, they had grown twice their size.

A chorus of Rover voices announced their mounting concern over this change in what they thought were only pretend dogs.

"Something's not right," someone commented as the wolves became even larger.

"It's that hermit wot did it."

"Somebody stamp on the slime."

Talk being just talk and not deeds amongst them at the moment, saw no one doing anything to stop the changes in the wolves from proceeding to their unknown conclusion.

Quickly, the familiar and petite forms of Whimper, Whisper and Wheezer, which had been known on a daily basis to Matthew and Evangel for six years, were transfigured to true wolf size. They became majestic and beautiful to behold. Evangel wanted to put her arms around all of them. She began to laugh with delight.

The wolves that they had become put fear into the men around them. The Rovers' fear became further enhanced when the wolves pawed at the ground and growled at the outlaws.

Tabard shouted at those around him, "Keep your senses, men. Put some arrows into em."

Those who had bows unslung them from their shoulders. They were in the process of nocking arrows when the wolves abruptly snapped into three separate and vertical streams of light. A sound like muted thunder accompanied this change. Three rivers of light billowed outward and upward further in rapid succession.

A feeling of lightning pulsed in the hermit's back yard.

Tabard was shouting like a madman, "Shoot them, you beef–witted codpieces! Stop them right now!"

He still had the presence of mind to grab one of Matthew's axes that was near the wood pile. He heaved it at the middle light.

A hand appeared out of the light and grabbed the hurled axe deftly by its handle. Hand, axe and the light were swallowed entirely by a tornado of greater radiance opening outward from its center.

Three whirlwinds turned upon their centers and grew to the size of the large trees at the edge of the woods nearby. A flame arose in the center of each vortex. Within each of these whirling gyres and within each single flame, the visage of a king materialized into visible sight. Brighter than the sun the light became until its illumination had a sound to it. Each tourbillion pealed out a trumpet like blast as if it had moved through a vast distance and the air of the world was displaced by its rapidity. Earsplitting in effect, it roared over them.

The concussion and tumult of these three entities made everyone in the yard go temporarily deaf.

Three great kings stared balefully down at them.

The one in the middle of the other two declaimed to them by thought, saying, *We serve the One who made us.*

The king to his left declared, *The One called I Am sent us.*

The third king disclosed, *The time of reaping is upon* you.

Men were besotted in stunned grief in being within the force of the three kings' presence.

Another, yet unseen, presence called forth:

"Some were whimpering in pathetic cries.
"Some were whispering in prophetic sighs.
"Some were wheezing in poetic replies."

Evangel approached the three before her with great respect and humility. "For the love I bear toward the three little ones that formerly stood where you stand now and for whom my grandfather and I protected and cared, how may I serve you?" she asked.

All three before her responded in unison, *We are Emissaries, Kings and Powers of the Risen One.*

The one in the middle of the other two became filled with a mighty force, *Strength, Honor and Freedom I bring to you from Him*, he said movingly.

The king to his left stated gently, *Mercy, Love and Grace I bring to you from Him.*

The third king directly stated, *Wisdom, Service and Healing I bring to you from Him.*

"For these gifts, brought to me by your kindness and might, I thank you," Evangel answered.

The three kings before her bowed their heads slightly in acceptance of her heartfelt thanks.

"Is it permitted, mayhap, for one as lowly as I am, to speak with you more?" she asked with trepidation.

The one in the middle nodded his head again, *Briefly, child, for our presence is needed elsewhere.*

"Will I ever see my wolves again?"

The one before her on her left nodded his head in affirmation of her question.

She hesitated to say anything else, thinking they would no longer respond any more to her.

Seeing, however, that they remained silently in place, she queried, "May my Grandfather be healed from this grievous injury done to him?"

The one on her right, shook his head sadly, "His sight is elsewhere now. This he understands and accepts, for what he has lost, he gains in abundance in other ways that those with sight can yet surmise. As I speak, his pain is gone. He protects you henceforth in those paths you will soon follow."

Evangel, waxing bold in manner, said, "This is distressing news for me to bear. Visible sight to him alights my heart in joy for he looks onto the world in great understanding and peace. Perchance, may I be given the boon of healing this humble man's wounds?"

Your petition is a fair and courageously stated one. For your love is exceedingly abundant, and as you have looked into the eyes of the Risen One, we leave the decision to heal him in your hands and in his heart.

Tears welled in her eyes even while gladness filled her spirit. "Again, I most humbly thank you for your kindness to me and mine."

Evangel turned away from the kings. Glancing at the men prostrate on the ground, she looked back at the mystery in front of her and asked, "What of these before you?"

What would you have of us do with them child of this world? asked the one in the middle.

"To punish them severely through harm or death to their person is fair for exacting

55

vengeance upon them for their violence against our kind."

The kings remained quiet, but seemed to lean toward her more as if in curiosity to hear her pronouncement.

"Yet to do so is but traitorous to the master carpenter who smote, in victory, the wood He was set upon."

What then is your decision, Evangel?

"I ask that they may be forgiven of their sins and henceforth serve me for as long as their strength may last and my service to the Risen Lord remains in pledge to Him."

All three great beings smiled.

The king to the right of the one in the middle laughed deeply and said, *So be it stated.*

The king to the left responded, *So be it finished.*

In reverse order in the way in which they appeared, they vanished. The kings disappeared. The single flame in each vortex shone brightly then went out. The cyclones wound down and dissipated their force completely. Instead of where kings, flames and tornadoes formerly turned in their places, now stood three silver gray and great wolves.

Muriel and Juliana stood transfixed, their eyes wide open and shining with wonder.

The mules they had tied securely three miles back were quietly eying everything from the edge of the clearing upon which The Refuge stood.

The Rovers, each to a man and one young boy, bowed in front of Evangel.

Tabard walked to her side, now in great diffidence and respect. He drew his sword from his side, saying as he handed it to her hilt first, "You have my life. Do with it as thou wilt."

"Nay, Master Tabard, this blade you keep for the service we step into together from this moment on."

"For one such as me, I deserve death," he said flatly and without emotion.

"You deserve life now, my Captain; you have lived in death for far too long."

Evangel walked over to the man she killed. She knelt down beside him. She placed one hand on his head and the other over his heart. "I ask forgiveness for my anger. I take it back and give it to the one who conquers the sting of anger. May the light of life blossom in him with the force of meekness. May the spirit of the one who vanquished death bring this mortal soul to his feet in this realm."

Dead no longer, the Rover at her feet arose. He bowed deeply and almost fell in doing so.

She steadied him on his feet with her right hand. "Tabard," she said softly to him, "Follow me to the man you tortured and blinded."

The Rover shrank back at her words.

She held out her hand to him.

He took it as though it was the most precious, yet puissant power in the universe.

Together they walked over to Matthew.

"Place your hands upon his head," she commanded.

"Grandfather, you have suffered more than anyone I have ever known in my life. I do not wish to see you so. May I, in the name of the Lord of Lords, for whom the three kings serve, restore the human sight of your eyes and heal, also, the wounds and affliction given to you unto this terrible day?"

"Child of my heart," answered Matthew, "I accept the judgment eked out on me by nature and the human soul."

"I would not have you thus, Grandfather."

"Already, as the king professed, I have seen my Lord with the eyes of my spirit and I am more than satisfied with my position in this life."

"Be that as it may, and as wondrous in truth as it is, I would have the light of your eyes alive with awareness upon what you look at in this world. It is, I know, but selfish of me. Will you grant the whim of a young woman who wishes you well?"

Matthew sighed and said, "It is in your hands, Jacquelyn Blessingvale, that I leave my life at your disposal."

She looked at Tabard and said, "It is you who must pray and restore him to what he was in order for him to be what he must become."

Tabard, leaving his hands in place where she had told them they must be, prayed in a voice that trembled slightly. "A man like me deserves nothing but the recompense he has earned in his wickedness. I do not understand what has overwhelmed me. It is like nothing I have faced before. I have done this man I hold now a great injustice. I deserve to die in his hands and, perhaps, he needs to slay me, in turn; or, in justice, blind me as I have done to him. Yet, I turn to this Risen One, who has forgiven me, and in his name, and for the young one here who I was going to rape, who calls me her Captain, I ask that if needs be, to slay me. I would fain be delighted for my life to be taken for his to be restored the way the Lady here requests."

Tabard hung his head low. He felt miserable and beyond any value. "This is a paltry prayer, Lady, and beyond my grasp."

"You speak truthfully, and powerfully, at last, Captain," she said.

She put her hands on his own and claimed, "So be it said."

Matthew, opening freshly restored eyes that shone with a more than human power, concluded, "So be it finished."

59

Tabard looked about him. Not a dry pair of eyes could be found in the hermit's backyard, except for the pair still sitting by themselves on a stump of wood where Tabard had first placed them there.

CHAPTER SEVEN

"Our fealty is sworn to the Risen One, and He, in turn, has promised us to be His own," she said to them. Evangel went to where the great wolves were standing. She bowed gently to them.

"In all these years in having you by our side, I loved you with all of my heart and protected you the whole time. I did not know that in doing so, you taught me many lessons. Indeed, I believe now that we were not so much taking care of you, but that you were taking care of Grandfather and me, instead."

She could see that they were listening intently to her. They were no longer small, cute and cuddly; their eyes reflected the force of wildness and the extreme intelligence of potent, prescient and perilous beings. An awareness shone from them that was singular in its presence. It was one completely foreign to mortals.

"When I found you in the woods close to the pool under the falls, it was God who sent me to you. With your mother and brothers and sisters dead around you, I felt that what had happened to me when I was a mere baby was a reflection of what happened to you at that time. Darkness is shattered by the light. Sometimes it overcomes it gradually. But conquered it is. The champion channeling such love may not be one pictured from the stories we hear as children. An old 'grandfather' saved me. And, a very small and young girl saved you."

One of the wolves looked up at the sun, sneezed and shook himself fully.

Evangel laughed. "Still, I think within all three of you live the wolves I used to know."

Walking to the wolf formerly called Whimper, she said, "The powers of Strength, Honor and Freedom were given to you by God. You have granted them to us through your love. I take these gifts and promise to use them in the spirit they were given you."

The wolf clawed the ground with one of its big forepaws.

She reached out and touched him on the shoulder. "Thank you for the time you have spent with us."

Evangel turned and approached the wolf once called Whisper. "The powers of Wisdom, Service and Healing were given to you by God. You have granted them to us through your love. I take these gifts and promise to use them in the spirit they were given you."

The wolf looked deeply into her eyes and walked over to Matthew where he sat down next to him.

The hermit bowed to the being in front of him, saying, "Always you guarded me when I slept. Little did I know what goodness and power were truly in your small form. I ask forgiveness for my ignorance."

The wolf lifted his head up and down at Matthew, as if to say that everything was just fine between the two of them.

Evangel said to the wolf by Greatworth's side, "Thank you for the time you have spent with us."

"Last," she softly stated to the one formerly known as Wheezer, "I stand before you. The one who was the smallest had my greatest adoration. I thought having you so close to me was good company for me. I understand now on this day that I stood in the company of a spirit filled with a great purity. I only hope that I was good company for you."

The wolf looked back at her steadily. A tear welled up in its right eye and dropped toward the ground.

Evangel caught it in her hand before it could land on the dirt in the yard.

"A royal tear from you is worth more than all the treasures of this world," she said to him.

Briefly touching the wolf under its chin, she declared, "The powers of Mercy, Love and Grace were given to you by God. You have granted them to us through your love. I take these gifts and promise to use them in the spirit they were given you."

The wolf approached her and with his nose against her left shoulder pushed her gently to the side.

"Thank you for the time you have spent with us," she said to him with a hesitant smile. She desperately wanted to throw her arms around his neck.

The three wolves walked to the center of the yard and stood in a line with one another. One, then the other, and finally the third, began howling. In an instant, they disappeared before everyone's eyes.

"What will I do without my little ones?" she asked to no one in particular with tears in her eyes.

CHAPTER EIGHT

Osbert Tabard took stock of what was happening around him in the backyard of The Refuge. He saw that Evangel, the hermit and the two older women were too emotionally spent and distraught over what had just occurred. *They need rest, even a brief surcease from the tensions this day has brought them.*

He also accessed the condition of his fellow Rovers. He saw that many looked haggard and worn out as well from the events that happened that day. The turmoil of going through the agonies associated with their former lives in light of the reckoning they received from the three kings to a new unknown one had also taken an equal toll on their spirits.

It's getting towards the end of the daylight, he thought, *best we at least stay here for the night. We can use some rest. After all, the hermit calls this place "The Refuge". From the look of everyone, we could use a safe place to stay.*

Tabard went over to Evangel and Matthew. He shared with them what he was thinking and what plans he tentatively derived from his review of everyone there.

Matthew looked over at Evangel. He, too, saw that she was overwrought. Turning back to Tabard, he said, "I agree with your summation.

We all need rest and time to come to terms with what has happened here and within our hearts."

"May we stay the night here, Sir?" Tabard asked charily, unable to look into the hermit's new pair of eyes.

"Please, call me Matthew. And, yes, kindly consider staying at least this night."

Evangel, who had been only half listening to their conversation, interrupted them, saying, "Good sirs, we will not be separating from one another, especially based upon what has just happened and to what we have been charged to do."

An inner light seemed to shine from her countenance.

Rovers started to gather around her, attracted by her renewed sense of energy and purpose.

She decided to address those present with her. "We are all exhausted by the labors of the day. All have borne afflictions cast upon them by this world's vast hunger for destruction and from its unquenchable thirst for peace to be ruined as well. Grandfather calls this forest God's Temple. Here amidst this peace and within the land The Refuge contains, we have the opportunity to learn more about what we must do to follow the path spread before our feet.

"Master Tabard, you are my Captain. I trust the plans you are making, but they are too small.

We have a new charge to follow, a new covenant to fulfill. Let us rest this day and evening. Tomorrow is almost upon us. When the sun rises the next day, perhaps we will put our thoughts together and see what will be revealed to us."

Tabard made sure that Matthew, Muriel, Juliana and Evangel took up quarters in the house. He also made sure that the sisters' belongings would be with them soon.

He had his men take the mules and secure them for the night. The animals were relieved of their burdens, which seemed strange to Muriel and Juliana because when the sisters had picket hobbled the mules, they had taken their packs off of the animals.

"Another mystery of wonder to consider," Muriel claimed, as she watched the mules being taken care of by several of the Rovers.

The objects stored in the packs were taken out, accounted for and put in their proper places.

Tabard had every Rover put what they had for belongings, as well as what they had pilfered from the Refuge, in the center of the wood splitting area.

They took stock over what they had in common with one another. Once they understood what they collectively had together, these possessions and belongings were stowed in various places throughout the camp, house and safe room. As Matthew had previously built several other sheds next to the house, these buildings easily accommodated their effects.

Some men volunteered to get more wood. Others offered to make several camping areas around the house so they were evenly dispersed around it. Sentries and pickets were formally organized. Shifts were assigned for the night. An evening meal was prepared and the food was apportioned fairly and sparingly among everyone.

After darkness had long been upon them, the camp began to settle down for the night. The Rovers' fires went out gradually. The first shift, consisting of three sentries, patrolled the area around the hermit's home, while four others positioned themselves at the points of the compass around the house in the forest nearby.

Quiet fully descended upon The Refuge.

CHAPTER NINE

Birdsong filtered down from the surrounding trees to those sleeping in the clearing below around the cabin. The light of day was just beginning to emerge from the gloom of night.

The men assigned to the third shift were halfway through their duty. The rest of the Rovers started getting ready for the morning ahead of them. Campfires were restarted, food was prepared and served. Excellent water from a fresh spring close to the house was drunk along with breaking their fast.

When the early morning rituals of getting ready for the day were completed, Tabard did not order his companion Rovers to make preparations for leaving The Refuge. Instead, he saw that his men took measures to expand the camp. They secured more wood for their fires, leaving the hermit's wood pile alone. They placed all of their weapons in front of them and made sure knives and swords were polished and honed to a satisfying and necessary sharpness. What armor they had was cleaned and burnished. Bowstrings were checked, as were the quality and supply of arrows remaining to them. Clothes needing to be mended were given to those with the skills to do so.

Menders and tenders, not so bad, thought Tabard.

An old part of him emerged, saying, *Listen to you: the new man.... You know, friend, you can't keep fooling yourself. You're still the same, or the old, you.* "Menders and tenders," *Truly, this new worship of yours has already reached its limit of reality. Your new you renders* you *a pretender.*

Tabard thought about this former aspect of his life only so far. He just stopped rationalizing about this message from his old self. The more he reflected on it, the less satisfied he became about believing its import to his current state of discernment. He let his mind rest and not struggle over conflicting interests.

He felt as though he was in a boat with a see–through bottom. The ability to look underneath the boat allowed him to observe what he was traveling over and moving through. He saw that attitude powerfully shaped the way he acted. His old disposition wanted him to attack other boats, to indulge without compromise in pillaging, ruining and stealing. Even if he were approaching a reef while chasing after such prey, he would not give a damn about it. It did not matter the cost of capturing, conquering and subjugating property and possessions that did not belong to him, the point was the hunger and desire for pure greed to hold sway in the center of his soul.

Guilt then has its sway over the actions you are fully aware you are taking. I was in a whirlpool of undisciplined desire for robbing and controlling people. It made me want to do worse things to people to the point where I could never go back to a normal *life. I guess I'm now starting to have a different hunger for something else now.*

Tabard's new inclination to follow Evangel's path made more sense to him. There was no longer any need to take material goods and lives away from people. There were far more lucrative and rewarding sources to find.

Perhaps it is as though I am listening to the voice of a demon talking to me.

Tabard shook himself.

"I have tasted and eaten illness. I forgot what doing so separated me from. A castle wall went up and I refused to go that way anymore. However, it took another whirlwind, three in fact, to carry me back to my senses."

But there is so much more that has helped lift me over that wall.

Tabard lost track of the time he spent wondering about the war between good and evil, the confrontation between the old man and the new one, churning away in his inner thoughts.

Within The Refuge, Matthew was the first one to awake. He had slept in his clothes on the floor in his study. Once awake and functioning somewhat, he prayed, and read for a while until all of the women were awake, dressed and preparing to break their fast as well. He joined them in the great room. He seemed dazed from the previous day's events as though he was still getting used to viewing the world around him with the new pair of eyes that had been given to him. Walking over to the fireplace, he stood before it lost in thought.

Muriel saw him standing there staring into the freshly lighted fire. Having great compassion in her heart about the suffering he went through the day before, she said, "Please, Matthew, have a seat at the table. I will be honored to serve you your food this morn."

Greatworth looked kindly at her, but with a start, for he had been simply gazing blankly at the hearth. Hearing her voice directed at him, he cleared his throat. "Thank you, Muriel. It is good to see you and Juliana here at The Refuge; for truly, this humble place is providing many people sanctuary this day."

Muriel pulled a chair out from underneath the table for him to use. She watched the old hermit slowly move to the chair and sit down with a deep sigh. "You have been, and remain, in my prayers, my friend," she offered him in a consoling voice.

Juliana, walking into the room, had noticed the difficulty Matthew was having in moving. "Good morning, Master Greatworth!" she exclaimed. "It does my soul good to see you hale and hearty this morn."

Brightening at her energy and heartfelt solicitation, Matthew responded, "Frail and flighty am I, rather, Sister Juliana. Yet, I thank you for your 'hale and hearty' greeting to me."

Neither woman further addressed their concerns about his wellbeing. Instead, they withheld any comment about them, trusting that the hermit's natural good health and fortitude would take over and help restore his old sense of serenity and composure once more.

Evangel entered the room laden down with bowls and plates.

Muriel and Juliana bowed with deep sincerity to Matthew and went to the larder to obtain the rest of the early morning's meal for all four of them.

Evangel opened the front door of the cabin. Sounds of the day, and from the Rovers going about their tasks and talking with one another, drifted into the interior of the home.

When everything was ready to eat and all four of them were seated at the table, Matthew stood

up and gave a benediction and prayer. He did, in
fact, seem suddenly transformed to them. His
words were straightforward and powerfully
stated, like the man himself. He began by saying,

> "What occurred here yesterday was both
> travesty and miraculous. The mockery
> capable of showing itself in man's heart
> was evident by all present, even by those
> causing such harm. The dark morality and
> dissipation of evil towards one another
> were shameful in their entirety.

> "The inexplicable intervention of the Lord
> by interrupting man's wickedness to his
> fellow man…is a mystery I do not
> understand, yet nevertheless, fully
> embrace. Little wolves becoming kings of
> the Lord, with powers in their hands
> surpassing the greatest armies that ever
> marched and fought on this world's soil,
> was a shock of divine intervention.

> "When I was disfigured and tortured, I
> thought with my mortal mind I was
> abandoned by God. That part of me gave
> up and died. Oddly enough, when my
> second eye was cut away from me, I gave
> up my life to heaven. When you three

became involved, I had no force left in me to rescue you. I was helpless.

"Still, three small wolves that I have taken for granted all these years as something ordinary, plain and of little consequence except for the small comfort they gave mostly to Evangel, were truly overlooked. God is with us all of the time no matter our feelings, fate or force of mind we bring to bear on whatever we think is common, not worth our notice.

"I ask for a blessing on everyone here, for the mules as well as for the insects, and birds. May the water and the food we eat, which nourishes us, be given an extra measure of grace for the purposes the Lord has set before us. May the forest and fields, rivers and streams nourish and protect us from further infamy. May the man who raised his hatred against me and inflicted his shame upon me be forever forgiven. May I, the greatest of sinners, yet walk in the peace, in the joy, and in the presence of the Lord."

When the hermit ended his invocation, the sun shone through the door onto him. Its light lit up his face and hands. What caused the greatest joy to the three seated around him was that his eyes were whole; the marks of pain were gone.

They ate together without saying hardly any words to one another, except for phrases like "Pass the bread, please," or "May I get any more water for you?"

Finishing their meal, Juliana stood up away from the table and said, "Please stay and rest yourselves. I will take care of everything here."

CHAPTER TEN

Evangel stood in the yard before them. Her back was to the front of the cabin.

New beginnings deserve being at a different side of one's home. A new day brings us to a new side of The Refuge. The old ways are in back of us, and the new....

She smiled at this thought. As soon as she did, many of them smiled back.

It surprised her. She was pleased with that reaction, especially when she started to consider the seriousness of the situation they had just entered. She decided the best thing for her to do would be to be positive.

After all, she wondered, *I have good news to share.*

"This can't look just a chore," she accidentally said aloud.

Some of them could not hear what she had stated. Several of them gave her a puzzled look, as if she were talking to them in another language they almost understood. Almost all of them wanted to hear what she had to say. They were eager to hear her opinion about the events they had all just experienced, especially on the day before.

She held back from speaking. She was waiting for something. Evangel realized she was waiting for three, little white waifs to run beside her.

I can't keep thinking like this. I'll be too serious and maybe even cry.

A cloud crossed over the face of the sun and temporarily darkened the light that had been streaming down so brilliantly just moments before.

In looking at her, they thought her still a child. Her hazel green eyes were steady, but somber in appearance. While she had attained a mature stature never observed before, she still very much had the innocence of youth clinging to her. She was small for her age, and had the look of a young boy when her hair was often put in braids that crisscrossed over the top of her head.

Her lush, thick hair was a deep red with golden streaks of blonde in it. When left free and unbound by a veil, hairnet, hat, wimple or even a metal circlet around her head, it had a tendency to fall over her eyes, which bothered and felt unseemly to her in the company of others.

The Refuge had never been filled with so many people. Hence, earlier in the morning before Matthew had arisen for the day, Murial had helped Evangel arrange her hair. The young maiden's hair was single plaited such that it fell over the right side of her shoulder. While it was also ribbon encased in its main braid, the rest of her hair had been taken up from behind and upwards again.

When the sun light again played on her face, the slight freckling she had ever since she was a little girl became even more enhanced than when she first stood before them.

Most people seeing her thought she was pleasant to look at. It was her energy and presence of spirit that made her exceedingly beautiful.

"What has happened here these past two days are surpassing mysteries and wonders. Yet, they are not just the result of a magician's illusion or a writer's play on words. This is no stage, but more like a coliseum where warriors battle with whatever monster, demon or champion the emperor wants to have play against the enslaved before him.

"You were known as the Dread Rovers, but I think of you now as God's Rovers. Just recently, you were known for your dread villainy and you turned your natural courage into false bravery. By pillaging others you stole from your own soul's treasury. Yet this raw daring and brazen boldness that you still have in you is part and whole of who you are.

"Perhaps we can consider you outlaws still, but for the Lord. The skills and courage you showed in being a worthwhile menace to this land are now transformed into making straight the way of the Risen One.

79

"I see us staying at The Refuge from the late spring to midsummer. We will rest our burdens, revive our spirits and make this our headquarters. We will then gather those to us who truly listen to the master's voice. Muriel and Juliana, you will return to the priory and share with them what we all have partaken and witnessed here. I want you to see how truly plentiful the spiritual harvest is before us and to share with me how best we can prepare for it."

She paused briefly, and looked directly at Tabard and the rest of his company of men.

"I have walked forth from the forest to free us from fear. You and I, being completely different from one another, have been bonded together for the purpose of setting the truth before the people around us who are lost in the slavery of false belief. From the experience of what we went through, you know many have such a limited view of life. The world to them is open to their own sense of plunder and selfishness. It is an endless cycle of spiritual gluttony because it ensnares people into a much smaller and narrower world. It confines them, it conforms them, and then confirms them to a material hell enslaved by the things they desire.

"We are not meant to live lives filled with this kind of poverty, having our base wishes controlling us like puppets." She stopped in mid speech. It was as though she were listening to another's voice and waiting to hear the full message.

Matthew and Tabard, hearing the choice of words she was using knew they were not only from a girl of seventeen years of age, but that she had been touched deeply by divine power. They—everyone present—could see her mind had been translated and transfused into knowledge and wisdom far beyond her years and life.

Evangel smiled, "Please forgive me if I seem too dramatic. I am merely a young girl who has been sheltered and protected in a refuge built by my grandfather as a place of meditation and peace. It is here that the tempest of man's selfishness was refrained from appearing. The world out there and the one I grew up in are the exact opposite of one another. Yet, even though I live in such beauty and innocence, I am still part of this other, baser world."

She paused again and frowned. "I miss my old life for it was the one I knew in complete surety. When I let down the walls of my heart, when I cast away my doubts and fears, I can see what lies ahead of us. It is a glorious vision beckoning us. Look what we have already seen. Instead of grievous death and hurt occurring to us here, we have been given their exact opposites. Life and healing. Life, to live more fully; and healing, to make this fullness possible and to become a living testament to His grace being upon us. I will follow Him because He has healed the contradiction between life and death, between understanding and ignorance and between fear and courage."

She became silent. Looking at them, she wondered for a moment if she had made any sense. She even thought, *Did I just speak in a different language?*

They still looked at her quietly.

Matthew came forward, asking Tabard to stand by the hermit's side.

Tabard bowed before the old man and to the young woman in front of him.

Gathering his thoughts together, the former Dread Rover said with great prescience, "We see that the continuation of the miracles that fell upon us yesterday is with us still today. Give these tidings anywhere in the Western Isles and I guarantee you people will flock to your side. I see you before a large host of warriors on the edge of the sea. Ships are below us, ready to sail for a kind of war that has never been waged before in our ken. I see a large banner held before you. It is a design containing three golden crowns. They are encircled in a field of deep blue. Around them are red and golden strikes of lightning beaming from the marks of royalty standing in its center. Four of them, at the compass points, are bigger in size and gleam silvery white in color."

"The Spirit of the Lord has allowed you to see what is already been foreordained," Evangel replied. "You, your men, Grandfather, and others will be there with me."

Evangel and Tabard, despite the obvious contrasts and experiences between them, looked equally haggard and exhausted.

Matthew said, "We must rest some more, and once rested make further plans for how, where and when we proceed to fulfill this calling."

As soon as the hermit finished saying the word *calling*, both mules standing alone in the back yard brayed at the top of their lungs.

Everyone laughed: relieved that it took only two jackasses to bring them back to reality.

CHAPTER ELEVEN

Osbert Tabard still was struggling to make sense of his new station in life. The old calling of violence still haunted him. It was a view of the world towards which he had been extremely attached. Constant strife and perpetual conflict were familiar patterns that were indelibly woven into his plan of mastery over other people.

His equivocation, or ambivalence, towards the new path he seemed to be headed on became more intense as the day passed. He became taciturn and aloof from his men. He kept brooding over this newly perceived awakening from the darkness he had so long inhabited. While he could feel strength pouring into him from his miraculous encounter with Evangel and Matthew, he began to see it also as a weakness, a vulnerability that seemed distasteful to him.

As Tabard did not want to be with anyone in his current moodiness, he went for a walk away from The Refuge. He headed into the woods without telling anyone where he was going.

Everyone's busy doing what they're supposed to do, he said to himself glumly. *No one's going to miss me for a while. Besides, what do they need me for, anyway? The old man has everything in hand. The girl of perfection has everyone on her mission.*

Even all my men, the Dread Rovers, now "God's Rovers", *are all getting comfortable making this place their new home.*

He could not believe that he had prophesied so blatantly and so eagerly earlier in the day. He was disgusted with himself. *Some form of drunkenness overwhelmed me and now I have this cursed hangover of doubt plaguing me.*

Tabard walked as one dejected and spurned by all of greater humanity. Realizing that he was becoming pitiable, he became even further morose and taciturn.

For several hours the Captain walked in the forest not paying any attention to where he was headed. The course of his steps took him through one of the darkest parts of the forest. He thought that the lack of light suited him better. Echoing the darkness around him, his temperament became more sullen and disconsolate. Rancor enveloped his mood. Had he a mind to notice it, the area he was passing through took on a dark and bitter cast. Gloom pervaded everywhere he looked. It shimmered and hummed irreconcilably in the background of his mind.

Looking up at the tops of the trees surrounding him, he involuntarily shuddered.

It took him—so it seemed—a brief amount of time to reach the end of this part of the forest. He walked out of it when he broached the edge of trees overlooking a vast depression in the land ahead of him. In the middle of this low lying area was a lake. Its surface was quite still, despite the wind playing on the wide variety of sedges, grasses and reeds that bordered it.

He decided that he would head down into the fen before him and see how close he could get to the water shimmering in the open light. Stepping down in the decline leading to the lake, he noticed movement on its shore.

There is someone down there, he observed to himself.

As his approach to the water got closer, and before he reached equal level with the rest of the carr, he saw that the man, *For he must be one,* he concluded, was carrying a large spear like object and was staring with fixed attention at the lake. Tabard thought the man must be fishing.

Curious to learn more about this individual, he picked up his pace. His state of mind began to change. Without knowing why, his moodiness and depression lifted toward a curious optimism. He pushed through pools of water, sedges and grasses, some of which cut his hands and face as he walked by them.

Going over a place covered with brown moss, he started laughing. Paying no attention at this point to where he was placing his feet, he slipped on a mossy rock underneath him. He fell into slimy, foul smelling water. Instead of becoming angry over this highly discomfiting and embarrassing incident, he became filled with a giddiness that surprised, and pleased, him.

Tabard picked himself up and got onto more secure ground. He felt as though he was close to being where the man he saw from the top of the ridge was fishing. He walked through thick clusters of what he knew as false acorus, or yellow iris. Oddly enough, they were blooming out of season. The three sepals of each plant collectively glistened in a yellow color that soothed his mind. He stopped to look at them more closely.

He thought he heard a voice in back of him give what sounded like a greeting. However, he next heard a man's deep voice say, "Seems we have a lover of flowers amongst us."

Tabard turned around and espied a tall man in deep crimson apparel. Like the flowers he was surrounded by, the man had a short, tufted beard. The spear like object he discerned from afar that the man carried turned out to be a pole weapon called a spetum. Oddly enough, the spetum and yellow iris had the same shape. While the plant had a three, petal–shaped flower, the weapon had a three–pointed, metal head that was affixed to the end of a seven foot pole. The center prong was at least a foot long. He realized that all three of these blades were quite useful for slashing.

When he asked himself, *Why would he be fishing with that?* his question remained unanswered because he immediately ignored it.

However, the heavily tattooed man looked at the three blades at the end of his weapon and admitted, "Yes, these here are not quite useful for fishing."

Tabard was taken aback, *Am I that transparent?*

As if hearing the Rover's thoughts, the man in dark red lightly laughed, saying, "No, I cannot hear your rumination to yourself. Although I am pretty sharp at surmising what people are thinking when they are near me."

Tabard was just about to introduce himself in order to learn who was so uncannily addressing him in such a manner.

"Come, come, my good man, let's move this conversation to my comfortable quarters. Follow me," the man in crimson commanded.

Tabard's expression went from surprise to compliance. He followed the man holding the spetum immediately upon his order to do the same.

"By the way," the stranger said to him, "My name is Sauria. I and my kind are Slayers."

It was getting dark by the time Sauria led Tabard to an encampment that was at the head of the lake, whose sources were a series of underground springs. Willows and scrub brush abounded as well as mosquitos, biting midges and black flies, all of which insects had been plaguing Tabard incessantly since he walked into the fen. None of these pests seemed to bother Sauria as none were around him.

When Tabard walked into this camp, he was quite a sight to see and smell. He was covered in mud, and blood trickled off his face, arms and legs from contact with the sharp plant leaves he had passed through to get to this point. He reeked from the slime and muck in whose ooze he had sunk in traveling across the many pools he went through to get to the side of the lake where he first encountered Sauria.

At least a dozen small campfires were burning. Four to five men were sitting around each of them having their evening meal. Other men walked through the camp on their own errands or on business for their brethren.

Sauria walked up to the only tent Tabard could see in the encampment. One of the two guards on either side of the entrance approached their leader, bowed and took his weapon, which one of the guards placed just on the inside of the fair sized pavilion. In being within smelling distance of Tabard, both guards wrinkled their noses in discreet disdain and disgust to the odor reeking off of him.

Sauria smiled noncommittally at them all.

Two other men brought over a well–made camp table, while another carried two elegantly built chairs in their wake. Once the table was placed just before the outside edge of the canopy leading to the front of the tent, the chairs were set across from one another at the table.

Tabard thought it curious that such a luxurious tent and furniture were present here in the middle of the wilderness. However, this thought raced through his head too quickly for further reflection. He wanted to hold onto and puzzle over it, but he soon forgot about this strange contradiction. Too much was happening to him all at once.

"Please," Sauria said to Tabard once the table was set for eating, "have a seat, as rough looking as it is."

Sauria's chair was pulled out for him by one of his men. The crimson clad leader beckoned his guest to be seated.

Tabard sat as he was bidden to do. "Thank you," he said to Sauria.

Food was brought and served to them.

Both men ate heartily. Tabard was astonished and pleased at the quality of the fare he was being given.

An ample amount of mead was poured for the two diners, to which Tabard helped himself liberally.

Upon completing the meal, Sauria sat back, folded his hands together on his lap and asked, "Was the meal to your satisfaction, my friend?"

Tabard quickly said, "Yes, Sauria, thank you; it was perfection itself, especially in this lonely area of the wild."

Sauria smiled at Tabard's words. "You are most welcome. But we find this area, on the contrary, to our liking. While we are indeed in the middle of the wild, we do not find it lonely."

Tabard looked down at his hands resting on the table. He did not know what to say to the man opposite him.

"Now that you have eaten...please excuse my incivility: would you care for some more to drink?"

Without waiting for a requisite answer, Sauria called for what the Captain thought was a special kind of mead to be served for the two of them. "Kindly serve us the entheogen," he commanded.

A bowl was brought from which the mead was poured into the glasses set before them. Tabard had never before seen the like of such elegant drinking vessels.

After being served, the leader asked for Tabard's name. "Now that you have rested from your labors and refreshed yourself at my table, I would like you to tell me your name and the reason why you came to the edge of the lake to see me."

Tabard, upon being questioned thus, answered without hesitation, "Kind sir, my name is Osbert Tabard, I am the leader of a small band of men call the Dr..., the Rovers," he corrected himself.

For some reason, he was having difficulty speaking.

The leader raised his cup to Tabard, but did not drink from it.

"We are encamped in an area near here," Tabard explained. "As my men were busy carrying on their assignments, I decided it was a good time to take a walk. I was deep in thought during my walk when I discovered this lake from the ridge to its west. I saw you and thought you were fishing. I then wanted to come see you."

Sauria urged Tabard to drink. The Rover took his glass in hand and raised it to his lips. Both men drank deeply.

Before his glass had a chance to go dry, it was filled again, and then twice more.

Sauria, drinking along with him seemed to be deeply contented. A smile played on his face frequently during their time together at his beautifully made table.

"Tell me, Osbert, what do you think of my *kap-no-batai*?" he asked discreetly.

Tabard tried to speak, but found that either his tongue had grown too thick, or he was just too exhausted to talk. He felt a great emptiness about him. Fear crowded close behind.

Covering his guest's discomfort, his host said, "I'm sorry, great chieftain of the Rovers, I forgot you do not speak but your own limited tongue. We call the ones who partake in this elixir *Those Who Walk in the Clouds*. Speaking of which, do you approve of it?"

Tabard still could not respond to Sauria aptly. To allay his uneasiness, *No*, he thought, *I am feeling on the borders of outright panic*, he managed to squawk a question out of him. "Whear rrr you from?" he tried to ask.

Tabard wasn't sure he heard Sauria's answer correctly. It seemed unintelligible to the Rover. Suddenly, he understood what he was saying.

"These men you see around you are my clade. There are almost a thousand of us here in your land. A hundred are here in camp."

Sauria pointed to the heavens and said, "We are from another set of islands over there."

Tabard tried to look where he pointed, but the man in red was not making sense. "Whas in this ink?" he yawped.

"This is our people's special liquid. It helps bring forth and generates the divine sources within us."

Sauria smiled. This time, though, Tabard saw fangs emerge from his mouth where his eyeteeth formerly were.

The Slayer stood up and walked over to Tabard, asking one of his men for a taper to be brought over to the table. When it was brought to him, he ordered the flame be put close to Tabard's face. Sauria examined the Rover closely. Satisfied with his cursory inspection, he nodded his head at the two guards who left their positions and went inside into the command tent.

They came out with a length of rope to which they tied Tabard securely. They took out a shorter length of rope and tied a series of concentric loops to the first rope where it ran down the Rover's back and under his groin.

A quarterstaff was brought to Sauria. He quickly slipped the staff through the loops. When he was done, two Slayers easily lifted the semi–conscious Rover up off the ground. He was carried over to an area that he had not been able to see previously when he was sitting at the crimson leader's table.

A small fire was going. Men were singing and chanting. The staff upon which Tabard dangled was slid over two other upright, forked branches that were already driven deeply into the ground opposite one another. Tabard hung over the fire on this crude spit while others drank, urinated on him and ridiculed the puny, helpless human that he was.

Gradually, he began to regain his wits somewhat. Still quite overtaken by what he had consumed, he could, nevertheless, make himself talk and be understood. He thought he was in a hammock aboard ship. Laughter greeted him when this comment was made.

Tabard kept blinking his eyes. They were watering terribly on him. For some reason that he could not understand, the crimson Slayer had the Rover's knife in his hand.

He even knows its name's Spinner. How can that be, did I tell em?

Sauria held Spinner in his left hand with great competence. As he flayed away Tabard's skin with consummate deftness, Tabard told the Slayer all that he wanted to know, and more.

95

CHAPTER TWELVE

They all spent the rest of the morning in relaxed company with one another. Introductions were made between the Rovers, Matthew and the three women. The men showed deference to Matthew, but gave their greater respect, even homage, to Evangel. She was uncomfortable with this show of esteem and withdrew herself almost exclusively into the company of Muriel and Juliana.

A hunting party was organized to go out the following day. They started their preparations in finding game by asking the hermit about his knowledge of the area around The Refuge. Matthew asked the three men not to hunt in the immediate vicinity, to which request they understandably agreed. Including a variety of water fowl, he told them about the best spots and game trails that they could try hunting for deer, elk, boar, quail, pheasant, and turkey.

After talking briefly with the hunters, Matthew went around to the other men to learn more about them and to see if he could be of any help to them spiritually. He spent the rest of the morning with the Rovers in this manner.

Many had great difficulty looking directly into the hermit's eyes. They could see traces of otherworldliness in them. Several of the Rovers thought they glimpsed a reflection of their own image, something that made them uneasy as what they saw was a different version of who they now were at that moment in time. Later on in the morning, when they had a chance to talk with one another about Matthew's appearance, they learned that some saw themselves as older or as younger than they now were when they looked into his eyes. What they found in common with this view of their identity was that they looked happier, more content with life.

Some of the fierceness and intensity that they had witnessed in the wolves' eyes after they were transformed back into the august animals they became still lingered in Matthew's gaze. As the morning waned, a look of great compassion and understanding appeared to reside in his eyes. Formerly brown in color, they were now a soft cobalt blue.

The three women spent the time making a tally of their food stocks. They organized themselves into an effective detail with Muriel coordinating their efforts. When the noon hour approached, they were in the middle of this task. Regardless of the tension and stress of the events they had just gone through together, they used this time not only practically, but lightheartedly, too. Laughter was often heard between them, yet they were accomplishing what they set out to do with great efficiency as well. Their levity was infectious and helped uplift the men in the camp.

Eventually, everyone stopped doing their morning tasks to prepare for the noon meal. With a crew of nine men, Matthew helped oversee putting together four temporary tables outdoors in the back of the cabin so that everyone could eat together at once. They used the two to three foot boles of wood for seats that Matthew had, with much labor, cut crosswise in anticipation of splitting them into firewood and for making kindling to help start fires in the cabin's hearth when needed. For tables, they brought out from one of the sheds rough planking the hermit had fashioned long ago for another shed he had planned to make, but never got around to building.

He was delighted with their progress and urged them to stay with him throughout the summer season so that he could get the work done he had been planning to finish for the past several years around The Refuge.

"It is true," he kept saying with pleasure and wonder, "many hands make light work."

Once the tables and "seats" were ready, food was served by the three women and four of the remaining Rovers. After those serving the food completed bringing it to the tables and were seated as well, Matthew blessed the food.

It was a good noontime break. Everyone was relaxed. All present enjoyed their time together at the tables.

Matthew stood up upon the completion of their fare. He asked that when the remains of the meal were taken away, if people could stay at their seats. He wanted everyone to take the time to talk about their situation and to make plans not only for the day, but for the time ahead of them and into the foreseeable future.

When the noon meal was over, everyone helped clear the tables. Clean up was swift and soon all of them were seated at the tables once more.

Again Matthew stood before the whole company. He made sure that everything was well with them, asking if they had gotten enough to eat and if they needed anything else that he could do to be of help to them.

Before he could say what he had planned to share with everyone, two of the Rovers stood up and addressed Matthew with their mutual concerns.

The Rover, who was brought back to life through Evangel's healing prayer, said, "I am concerned about the whereabouts of Captain Tabard. Some of us, I know, have not seen him since the early morn."

The young boy, Colin Hays, who had been holding the rope secured to Matthew's neck the day before, said, "I saw the Captain walking around here in the early morn. But he was quite gloomy. He seemed bother by something cause he wasn't talking to anyone and he just skulked around. I saw him last walkin into the woods. Did anyone see em at all leavin, or seen em since?"

Several other Rovers said that they had seen him walking around the camp in a perturbed humor. It was discovered that only Colin had seen Tabard walk out of the camp.

The man who spoke first after Matthew, Terric Lovell, asked of Colin, "What direction did you see the Captain leave, Colin?"

Colin pointed to the east.

Lovell looked at the hermit and said, "It's not like the man to just get up and leave."

"I've never known him to do that either," said Colin.

Murmurs of agreement broke out amongst the men.

"You know your leader far better than I, Terric. What do you suggest we do?" Matthew asked.

"What do you say, men?" Lovell queried. Men's voices could be heard discussing possible actions to take. Soon, one of the three men who had held down Matthew the day before in the wood splitting yard stood up.

"Just to be sure you know me, those whom I've just met that is, my name's Óengus Scanlan. I saw the Captain leave as young Colin said. I followed him for a bit without his knowin. Course it weren't nothin to follow him cuz he weren't payin no attention to nothin round him, includin me."

Putting this new information together that Scanlan had just shared with what everyone else had said, Lovell quickly responded by asking him, "Could you take several of our best trackers with you to the last place you saw the Captain?"

Scanlan nodded to Lovell that he could do that.

Everyone looked next at Matthew, waiting to hear what he might add or suggest.

"I think that we should wait a little while longer," he recommended. "We may just be too anxious about the Captain, seeing as how we have just been through so much in the last day. Captain

Tabard is a very capable man ordinarily, isn't that right?" he queried them.

A unanimous assent was given back to Matthew by Tabard's men.

"Let's wait till mid–afternoon," Greatworth suggested. "If he has not returned, we can send three patrols out. Each one will have three men in it. The three best trackers among you will lead each patrol."

"Your plan has solid merit, Matthew," Lovell answered. "What else are you thinking?"

"Ten of you will be actively looking for the Captain, with Óengus being the tenth Rover. I would fain go with you as I know these lands around here to a great length. Alas, my age would only delay you. That means another ten of us are left here. If I may, with your permission, I will stay here in the front of the cabin waiting for you.

"In case he returns from another direction, we'll place two rings of people each at varying distances from the cabin. The outer ring will have four people in it, while the inner one will have five. The fifth person will have one runner who will communicate with one another and with me. Each person can move back and forth in their piece of the circle, which can be determined once the "rings" are in place. The inner ring will move around the cabin from east to west. The further ring will move in the opposite direction.

"If he does come back while you are gone, I will send runners after you to let you know that he has returned to us."

The hermit's suggested strategy was accepted by all.

Men for the three tracking patrols were selected, as were those who were to be in the two rings around the cabin.

Lovell stood and proposed they leave earlier than the middle of the afternoon. "It's important we have as much light as we can to track his movements," he offered. "We should leave no later than noon."

"Noon it is then, Terric," agreed the hermit.

Colin stood and asked Matthew, "Are there any people, or animals around here, that would attack a man alone in the woods?"

The hermit smiled at the question, but then realized it had a basis of tragic truth to it. "For a long time, my son, and within my memory, these woods have been safe."

Greatworth frowned, "Yet, there was a time before this cabin was built when one ventured out, especially alone, with great trepidation."

The hermit went silent, self–absorbed in his memories of that time.

Evangel eventually urged her grandfather to explain more about this time to them.

"Some distance from here, in the direction Óengus told us Tabard headed, there is a great woodland fen. I doubt the Captain could reach it in the time he has been gone because it is a good four to five days walk from The Refuge." Matthew broke off what he was going to say.

Colin, seeing the old man give a strange, worried look toward the east asked the hermit, "What is it, Master Greatworth, that concerns you about this place you mention to us?"

Matthew looked at him and the rest of the company before him. "It was rumored that strange lights, voices and ill events overtook mortals when they went into the area of the shores along the lake that is in the center of the fen. People went missing. Sounds of combat were often heard, with men screaming in battle rage and in mortal fear from wounds received and visions seen. Those who came out of this place were forever changed."

"How were they so changed, Matthew?" Juliana questioned him.

"They had both a haunted and hunted look about them. When it became night, they often could not be consoled because of the fear they felt consuming them. They demanded that a light be next to them during the whole time of evening's darkness. Normal prayer did not help soothe the level of their dread, either. Sometimes, people who were gifted at driving sickness, demons or ill spirits away from the minds of these folk, would need to be summoned."

All of them fell silent after hearing what Matthew had said to them.

Lovell stood again in their midst and asked, "Let us prepare ourselves for this venture, for I fear for Tabard, and for ourselves if this fen be fraught with evil again as it was so long ago."

Everyone agreed to this last comment.

The sun moved in its arc overhead. There was no sign of Tabard. All too quickly, it became the time Lovell suggested that they head out with the tracking parties.

The plans that were derived from their discussion in their morning council about the Captain were now put into effect.

Three patrols, nine men, followed Scanlan as he headed due east away from the cabin. They were provisioned for six days and carried waterskins with them. In the early afternoon, Matthew had drawn a rough looking map of the area east of The Refuge. It was sketched out on the dirt near the wood splitting block in the backyard of the cabin. The hermit wanted to be sure they had their bearings straight, as well as a geographical fix, on where they might be going in relation to their present location.

The wind picked up in its intensity as the men followed Scanlan out of the Refuge.

Evangel ran over to Matthew, asking him, "Grandfather, please say a blessing and prayer over this mission before these brave men leave the sanctity of this favored place."

"Yes, child, this is a wise suggestion to follow," he replied.

The hermit hailed the Rovers who were beginning to disappear from the sight of the cabin yard. Hearing Greatworth call them, they paused and waited for the old man and young woman to gain their side.

When Matthew told them Evangel's plea for prayer, they immediately agreed. Some men took to their knees, others bowed their heads, and some looked steadily at the hermit as he said his benediction and prayer for protection over them.

The wind soughed dolefully through the tree branches as he appealed for help.

At the conclusion of his petition, Matthew opened his eyes and saw everyone remaining in place. Realizing their unstated intention, he asked Evangel to pray as well.

Evangel humbly stood forth and raised her head to the sky above her, saying,

"I am but a simple being. I have no depth of experience in this walk of life. I am untried in the ways of the world. I only have this life that God has given me. I am but a silly girl, burdened with the weight of girlish thoughts. Yet, The Lord has seen fit to pour His grace upon me. Our Captain is in a struggle over the peace of his soul. I have seen the conflict being waged over his path's direction. I ask that the power of this struggle be turned to his goodness, to the hope of his better angels; that he be returned to us hale and in the power of his youth and in the grace of the Lord's mercy."

Men, many never having completed a prayer in their lives, intoned, "So be it said."

Greatworth concluded with the corresponding phrase, "So be it finished."

Matthew and Evangel watched the men disappear into the trees. Grandfather and granddaughter returned to the cabin and waited until Matthew thought it was appropriate for those remaining behind to place themselves around the cabin in the encircling two formations.

Scanlan led the tracking patrols deeper into the woods.

CHAPTER THIRTEEN

It was early morning of the next day. The water in the lake was turbulent. Wind was racing over it in rapid gusts. Waves crashed against the shore where Tabard lay naked. He was stretched partly out on the sand and on a patch of brown moss. There was a bitter taste in his mouth.

Without opening his eyes, he turned over on his side and retched a vile fluid out of his mouth. He thought it would never stop coming out of him.

When the vomiting was over and he began dry heaving, he got on his knees. He had serious trouble trying to stop the convulsions still racking his body while trying to breathe at the same time.

He struggled to inhale just one breath of air and failed. He passed out, and breathed naturally on his own at last. The Captain slept this way until noon.

Tabard awoke once more. The wind had died down substantially and with its cessation, the lake lay peacefully before him.

He tried standing. Unsuccessfully. He sighed. Cautiously, and with great concern it would not work, he took a deep breath of air and gladly welcomed it into his lungs. It felt like water drunk by a man parched with thirst in the midst of a craven desert.

He shortened his goal in trying to stand on his feet. Instead, he managed, just, to get onto his knees.

When he opened his eyes and tried to look around him, the intensity of the light on his eyes blinded him. He almost passed out again.

Gradually, the world stopped spinning so dizzily around him. The whirring sound that had accompanied this spell of vertigo lessened, slowed and slipped away from him.

He managed a smile, which, had he the capacity to see, looked more like a snarl instead. He remained on his knees and did not throw up on himself or dry heave his way into unconsciousness.

The Rover heard the soft rustling of leaves in back of him. When he opened his eyes to look at them, he found that he was in front of a stand of old willow trees. Though there was no wind, the branches swayed slightly in cross-rhythm to something moving them.

He did not have the capacity or energy to try reconciling why they were moving without a cause he could not see. He endured this anomaly and the faint laughter he kept hearing, not out of a reserve of strength. He had none. The laughter was not merely derisive; its very own resonance seemed an insult to his sense of being human. He endured the feeling as an animal would while its owner whipped it.

He closed his eyes.

Time passed.

A complete thought finally came into his mind: *I am alive.*

Scanlan led the three tracking patrols to the point where he had last seen Tabard.

Careful not to muddle any signs of Tabard's passage through the forest with their own tracks, they laid out a grid the three groups could employ in finding their Captain's trail. The best tracker in each group led point. Two men per group flanked each man on point ten feet behind their respective leader. Each group covered a radius of fifteen, for a total of forty-five, feet between them all.

It was in the middle hour of the afternoon when one of the trackers came across their Captain's footprints.

111

"He's not payin attention to where he's headin. See," he pointed out to the others after calling over to everyone and they converged on the track he had found. "He's wanderin back and forth."

"Aye," another tracker agreed. "But he's still walkin in an easterly headin from what I can see from here."

The lead tracker turned to Scanlan, "Thank you for your alertness in watchin the Captain head out of camp. No point in keepin with us. Turn round n head back to The Refuge. Inform Matthew we found Tabard's trail. We'll take it from here. May the words of the hermit and the girl be fulfilled with the promise of finding the Captain whole."

The tracking parties headed out with their quarry's trail held fast in their keen sight.

Óengus retraced his steps to the cabin and relayed to Greatworth what he had seen and that the Captain's trail had been found.

The Captain, not feeling at all like one, tried to remember what he was doing here in this spot. When his mind attempted to bring back the night before, he felt it flitter unsteadily away from any memory of it.

He stopped trying to anchor his mind onto something that did not cooperate with him in doing so.

What in my mother's womb is going on? Tabard took a try at standing. He fell down. Three times.

The fourth try was somewhat successful. While he was able to stand like a human being, he did so as though he was still drunk, drugged, damaged, or any combination thereof.

Perhaps thrice.

Eventually, he found that he was able to explore a little bit of the area in which he found himself. There were no indications that anyone else but Tabard had been there.

This lack of any presence other than himself disturbed him. He could not understand why it did. Deeply. Profoundly. He shrugged his shoulders in dismay. Then he shuddered as if something wanton, even evil, passed over him.

He found his clothes folded not far away on the beach in neat rolls on top of one another.

Gratefully, he got dressed. Clumsily.

Sitting down to put his boots on, he discovered Spinner was in his left one.

Holding it in his hands, he took it out of its sheath. He trembled. Unbidden, he saw himself in some dreadful, nightmarish position over a fire, and almost fainted once more.

His skin tingled as though a knife edge had gone over it lightly.

113

Sheathing the knife quickly, he put his boots on, stood up and looked at a ridge above him in the distance.

For some reason he could not fathom, he started to go that way. The farther he walked towards it, the more confident he felt in heading in its direction.

He kept his mind free of any serious issues. He hummed a song to himself that he had heard when he was in a tavern on the eastern side of the vast island archipelago through which he had traveled most of his adult life so far.

"Ah the doxies here are free.
They shimmer not with gold,
but make us laugh with glee.

"I always thought them so bold:
when three went to hold me
and spent my passion fourfold.

"Ah the doxies here are free.
They shimmer not with gold,
but make us laugh with glee."

He sang this familiar, sailor's shanty with gusto. However, as he kept repeating it and adding improvised and salacious versions to its melody, he became less enthusiastic in belting out its tune.

Tabard stopped singing in mid verse when he walked into a large clump of yellow iris.

False acorus, came its name to him.

Tears, unasked for, rained down his cheeks.

Yet, there are no yellow petals here.

He was glad there were none. He shied like an abused horse about to be beaten when an image of the flower came to his mind. For a brief second he thought he saw a three–pronged weapon with a beard underneath its metal head.

He quickly tried to sing the shanty again.

Can't. Try for another. Failed.

Moving further into and then running as fast as he could move through the large patch of young, yellow iris plants, he placed his foot on a stone festooned with slime and lichen.

He slipped....

And fell into a pool of ooze whose mire stank like a foul drink of mead. His chest landed squarely on the top of the rock.

Everything squeezed shut on him.

Tabard, without recognizing the import of the image, saw a man in dark red. A contemptuous smile was on his face.

"Care for another drink, my wry one?"

Though his words seemed cast in a low baritone of phrased innocence, sheer dread entered into the Captain. They drenched him in utter anguish.

The Rover crawled out of the pool. He stank. He reeked. His mind whirled, and filled with chaotic visions as well as the stench of his own blood.

He heard more laughter, and chanting once again.

A knife flashed in the light of a fire.

Flames of unconsciousness reached into him. He stopped knowing who he was. He was simply another plant swaying in the breeze of his illusions.

Unawares, his body saved him again as it had on the lake shore when he became unable to breathe naturally. His muscle memory scrambled out of the ocean of his doubts and fears and saved him.

Tabard, or at least the physical thing that he had become, walked out of the fen and onto the path leading up to the ridge above him.

He collapsed there. He was giggling. Snot flowed from his nose. The Captain then soiled himself, and well.

116

The trackers made camp for the night. They had followed the impress of their Captain's footprints and any other spoor or signs of him they could detect until they could not see them anymore due to lack of light.

They made a rough camp. All of them ate sparingly. Three of them volunteered to set a watch over the others in three shifts. The trackers not on watch fell asleep slowly. When they did finally fall into the arms of their dreams, they were disturbed by the images brought to them in their sleep. They thought they saw men in dark red. Singing. Chanting. Looking at them and smiling, lizard like, while they skinned the carcass of a man resembling Tabard.

When they opened their eyes in the morning, the dreams seemed lost, forgotten.

They broke their fast reluctantly. No one was hungry.

Yet the remnants of a dread cantillation kept ringing in the background of each of their minds as they again resumed their task in finding Tabard.

It never let go of its thrall over them.

They travelled five days more like they did the first one. Their dreams became worse. Their

117

sleep became a contradiction: instead of getting rest from it, they became more exhausted.

Rest was meant to be a place of restoration, not perdition.

They spent the sixth day in a stupor. No one ate. No one kept watch. Their water was gone.

———◆—►

Óengus found them in a funk of forgetfulness. He yelled at them. Pulled them to their feet. Slapped their faces until they became filled with anger at his blows.

The Rover had them drink the water that he carried in a water skin whose precious liquid was obtained from the hermit's spring.

Their eyes, opening in the light of awareness as they gulped the blessed water, showed they were gaining some sense of strength at last.

Scanlan fed them dried jerky. He sang to them. Told them jokes that were stupid, silly, lewd and audacious in their insight into the human condition.

The nine men slowly recuperated from their listlessness.

The seventh day they began tracking again in earnest.

Before they began their search, the lead tracker announced, "Accordin to the rough chart the hermit drew for us of this area, I believe we're close to the edge of the fen."

"It has to be so," Óengus said. "The closer you've approached it, the more you were stopped in doin so."

The men greeted this observation in grim silence.

"How much of the Grandfather's water is left us?" one of them finally asked.

"Half," was the response.

The lead tracker sighed.

They waded forth into a thick wood as though encountering an invisible stream of water flowing against them. Midway through the press of their push through the depth of this part of the forest, Scanlan stopped them. He became worried because their eyes were losing their focus once more.

He had everyone, including himself, take a drink from his water bag.

"We have to get back into our three groups. Each member of the group must tie himself off to another, as though we were on board ship in a storm, or in a blizzard on land in the dead of winter."

"This feels like the dead of summer," one of the men responded.

"Aye, and it feels like death is breathin on us," another man said in disgust.

Óengus ignored the men's comments. Ropes were unslung from the shoulders of several trackers and shaken out onto the ground. He checked to see that each man had securely tied himself off to each of his fellow team members.

To the lead tracker, he asked, "Do you know where the Captain's trail leads?"

"I do," was his answer.

"Show me," Scanlan demanded.

The tracker pointed directly in front of him.

Óengus tied himself to the leader, saying, "Okay, I will start in the direction you just showed me. If you can, and I wander away from the correct heading, flick the rope to the right or left for the right way to go. Do you understand me?" he asked.

"Yes," came back the response.

The Rover looked into the eyes of the tracker. Somewhat satisfied with the amount of awareness still present in the other man's expression, Scanlan took the front position of his woebegone column of men. He led them forward to find Tabard.

After much effort, and in a slow–motion fog of movement, they broke through the trees and gained the edge of the ridge.

Scanlan gave them all another drink of water.

One group of men did not want to go further.

Scanlon chose not to argue with them. He made them stay in place and tied their lead tracker to the last tree leading onto the ridge. He tied a complicated knot that would have to be diligently cut with a sharp knife blade, or by the swipe of a sword edge, to undo it.

With the two groups of men left him, they moved forward and descended down the trail. The fen spread out below them.

Scanlan yelled at them not to look at it.

He did something he had not done since he was a young child. He said a prayer. Out loud.

At first, it was swallowed by the doubt of the men he was leading. That collective sense eventually melted away. Next, the potency of his praying was dulled by the fetid odor and fear wafting up to them from below. It was difficult to keep his petition going, but he felt the resistance against him falter and then fall away from all of them completely.

He saw that they had stopped. Somehow he got everyone going again.

They reached the Captain where he had fallen in the middle of the path. Without knowing of Tabard's presence, all but the last man in line passed him. This one happened to fall on top of his leader, which succeeded in completely stopping his own group of men. As the lead group was also tied to the second one, they came to a stop as well.

Óengus felt the rope tied to him jerk him to a halt. He had enough awareness left to see the reason why they all had wavered to a stop. He went back and had two men lift the Captain up and carry him back toward the top of the ridge from where they had descended.

With relief, he found that as they retreated from the fen, it was easier to concentrate and to be aware of what they were attempting to achieve.

They gained the ridge.

The tracking party left behind simply stared at their companions blankly without knowing who, or what, they were. Scanlan gathered them together with the rest of the men.

The Rover had two men put together a makeshift litter from fallen branches. They tied two of their cloaks onto it, using a third to provide strips of cloth to secure the cloaks to the branches.

Managing to carry their leader into the depths of the thick wood successfully, they stopped within its safe embrace. They undid the ropes they had tied to one another, for their senses had returned. The feelings of bewilderment and numbness had melted away from them.

Nine hardened, but humbled men, thanked Scanlan for his leadership, resolve and strength in keeping them on their mission in finding and retrieving their Captain. They also thanked him for rescuing them as well.

When they went to examine their Captain more closely, they did not recognize him, at first.

They saw a man, emaciated, bleeding and without awareness of who he was. When Tabard at last opened his eyelids at their repeatedly calling his name, both eyes were pure white, like the hair remaining on his head.

CHAPTER FOURTEEN

When they finally returned to The Refuge, the rest of the company was eagerly waiting for them. The tracking parties had been gone for eleven days. During their absence, the others had been busy. Extra garden space had been made. Crops were planted. Hunting parties had successfully found game, which in turned had been butchered, salted and was in the process of drying.

Muriel and Juliana had gone back to the priory. They left the mules behind to be of help in all of the varied tasks that such beasts of burden can accomplish.

Besides, Muriel thought, *they are needed more with Matthew than at the priory where there's a growing pack of mules there.*

The hermit sent two of the Rovers to accompany them. Once they had guided the sisters back to St. Åyrwyus Priory, the men were to proceed onto Dawn's Abbey, the monastery that was located another day's journey farther on.

Upon conferring with everyone remaining at the cabin, it was decided to have the women and men talk with both of the holy orders respectively. They were to relate the incredible events that had just occurred at The Refuge. Matthew understood that the clerics' reception to such news was important to discover. It would help him determine, literally, where their next steps might take them.

He did not think that the monks or the sisters would receive this information willingly.

As a matter of fact, he thought, *I believe both orders will be hostile to it.*

The hermit predicted, however, there would be a few who would accept this great testimony and draw near to The Refuge to learn more.

Perhaps these folk will want to study these events and meditate on their significance to amplifying their faith.

Greatworth also knew that once this covenant of new faith was announced throughout the land there would be a rush of more people to support it.

Of course, he knew, *there will be a backlash to it. Most likely violent.*

Aloud, he commented, "We must needs take our knowledge to all classes of people and to those in all the walks of life in which they live and labor."

As the old man puzzled over these issues, his deliberations were interrupted with the news that the tracking parties had returned. He went out to greet, hopefully, eleven men. He was so eager to talk with them, he did not think to inquire if Tabard had been found and brought back.

Believing they were already in the front of the cabin, he went out with a greeting on his lips. To his surprise, no one was there. Listening intently, he heard voices and excited conversation coming from the back of the building. He ran to the backyard area.

When Matthew arrived at a trot into the wood splitting area, people looked up at his entrance in the yard. They registered surprise at his being so spry. Many smiled and greeted him.

"Where are they?" he asked out of breath.

"They are yet on the trail walking back here on which they left to find the Captain," informed Colin.

Terric, anticipating the hermit's questions, said to him, "They are about a mile out from us. Scanlan sent a runner to inform us of their being here soon. And, yes," he added, "they are bearing a man on a litter with them."

Even though they were drawing very near to the cabin, Matthew was disappointed the tracking parties had not yet arrived at his doorstep.

His optimism returning, he announced, "It is well and good that they are nigh and not yet present with us. We must use this time before they get here to make arrangements to see to their comfort."

With subdued excitement, he asked people to get the tables ready for a meal. They brought out plates and cups and went to the spring to ensure there was plenty of fresh water to have on hand for them.

"I am sure that they are famished, parched and weary from their journey," he declared to them all.

In everyone's elation over, and during the ensuing commotion in preparing for, their return, the runner who had reached The Refuge and told his companions that the parties would soon arrive, was ignored.

Everything was in order to the hermit's satisfaction when the lead tracking party emerged from the woods.

There was stunned silence when the company in the yard fully looked upon the condition of the men entering the area. No one recognized them as the hale and hearty men who left them. In truth, they did not recognize them at all. The other men walked as though they were not there. When they looked at their fellows, they looked past them. They had a fixed stare that Matthew knew well. It was the veteran soldier's gaze after being exposed to the extremities and horrors of war.

It isn't as though their eyes are empty. They are too full, overflowing, there's too much to see that cannot be accounted for....

"What has happened here?" he asked worriedly, as well as with a bit of petulance over the fact he could not have been of help to them.

The second party entered the clearing. They were in worse shape. For they, and the third one behind them, were the ones who forged down the ridge path and rescued their Captain. They walked in rote, automatic steps.

Matthew inhaled deeply with worry, *They have been spelled*, he said to himself.

Evangel arrived in the yard. She had been working in the garden and had been the last to learn of the Rovers' return.

She, too, wondered aloud, "Are these our men, Grandfather?"

The hermit did not answer her query to him.

The lead tracker for the third party limped into sight. Behind him were the other two trackers who were carrying a litter. Upon it was a stick figure of a man. Beside the roughly made stretcher walked Scanlan.

Scanlan they knew. However, he had spent the least amount of time away. But even he looked aged, careworn and beyond weary. His eyes were aflame as if he were under a raging and strange delirium.

In a commanding voice, Greatworth called out, "These men have been exposed to an eldritch power and need our aide. Bring them into the center of the yard."

When all eleven men were in the center as they were bidden, and the remaining company had surrounded them, Matthew gently asked the two litter bearers to place their burden on the table next to him.

Other men went to help lift their burden, but the hermit shook his head, *No*, to prevent them from interfering with the last part of the mission these trackers had taken upon themselves to complete.

"Prithee, kindly help seat our companions. Some may need to lie down. Place them on the tables so that they are up off the ground," Matthew urged.

Five trackers were able to sit down. The first three men, who had entered the clearing to The Refuge, stretched out prone on the tables around their Captain.

Matthew walked over to where the lead tracker and Scanlan stood next to Tabard.

With great effort, the tracker placed his hand onto Scanlan's left shoulder. In words no more than a whisper he said, "Had you not sent him back to us, we all would have failed this mission and been forever lost."

Matthew took one, then the others by their shoulders and individually helped them get seated.

As arranged before they arrived, food and water were brought to the tracking party. The more than exhausted men refrained from eating. It was the water they wanted.

Terric made sure they did not drink all of it down too hastily.

Attention turned to the man still lying in a litter, but now resting on a table.

"Is this our Captain?" asked Colin with alarm.

No one answered him.

Scanlan, hesitantly at first, then with more assuredness, told them the events that had overtaken them and the unearthly war they had endured in rescuing the strange figure lying down in front of them.

Not once was his report interrupted.

When he finished, silence reigned. The sun's rays shone upon them. All but one in the tracking party looked up gratefully at its light and warmth beaming down upon them.

Matthew stood next to the one rescued whose hands had been placed one on top of the other over his stomach. The hermit placed his own warm hands onto those before him.

His hands are radiating the cold flames of death, he thought.

Greatworth wanted to let go, but he held onto them. As the cold in the strange looking man's hands seeped into his, Matthew sent a surge of warmth back.

The lead tracker, whispering again, said, "No words have passed from his lips since we found him and carried him here to you."

The hermit prayed a brief prayer for discernment and words of wisdom. *Yet*, he thought forlornly to himself, *this man is far beyond my humble reach*.

Evangel walked over to Matthew's side, hoping that she could at least offer silent support to those around her. She stood in between the sun and the wasted man's face in the stretcher.

He shrank away from her when her shadow fell upon his countenance.

People near him jumped in alarm at this reaction.

Tabard uttered the first words the trackers had heard him speak. "I am ashamed," he moaned. "I have failed you, Lady."

CHAPTER FIFTEEN

Evangel, fully realizing the import of what was just said to her, shrank back from the old looking man lying before her. Realizing that her resolve to be strong in the face of this man's great infirmity was weakening, she mentally shook off her fear and leaned again over the litter.

She touched Tabard on his cheek and said, "Nay, it is I who failed you. For I lifted a prayer up to the heavens for you to return to us fit, hale and hearty. Yet, I see you are compromised at best in your health upon your return here. The lack of merit is upon my shoulders, not yours."

"Lady," Tabard insisted, "the fault does not rest upon your shoulders, but upon my duplicity and inability to be constant toward your faith in me."

"You must save your strength, Captain. Perhaps the burden of what has befallen you should be borne by both of us."

The Captain coughed as if he were compromised by old age. Letting go of one of Matthew's hands, he touched her on her wrist.

She saw that his hand was shaking as if he were in a palsy.

Tabard said, "If I had any tears left in my body, I would spend them on the men here who rescued me. Their suffering for my cause is not only in the physical realm..."

He paused to catch his breath, "and it greatly aggrieves me."

Matthew gathered the Captain's hands back into his own. "You must rest now, Captain. Soon, we'll have you back on your feet and you can help us build The Refuge into a place that truly will live up to its name."

The leader of the Rovers shook his head and tried getting up on his elbows. Too weak to accomplish this simple task, he fell back onto the litter. His face turned red, then mottled in color. Looking directly at Greatworth, he whispered, "I have compromised the safety of everyone here."

Matthew spoke to those around him. "We need to empty the biggest shed and make room for these four men lying on our tables. Our efforts should go toward restoring the health of all those in the tracking party. Once we get the infirm in the shed and comfortable, we need to start enlarging our living space, too."

The lead tracker approached Matthew and said, "He believes he failed the Lady and that he has betrayed the sanctuary of this place. In going up against the unknown and unseen, we can only describe what our battle was to reach him and bring him back to you. We cannot imagine, therefore, the depth and horror of what the Captain was exposed to even more than ourselves."

The hermit looked at the other man and asked, "Pray tell me once again, what is your name?"

The man smiled despite his obvious exhaustion and weakness. "William Valarin," he answered,

"Thank you, William. I know that you have important news to tell me. And you will have the chance to do so. Right now, though, it is best you get some rest. Later on in the evening, or early tomorrow morning, I want to hear everything you and your men know. And, don't know."

Over the next several days, the men at The Refuge were quite occupied in expanding the living quarters available to them. The large shed where the most critically ill and exhausted trackers, including Tabard, were kept was made into a four–season building whose express purpose was in taking care of them. The shed was expanded to fit eight to ten adults needing medical care and nursing. They called it the Mercy Shed, although it became far more substantial looking than a mere outbuilding.

Three men were sent to Trabaile, which was the closest town near them. Located on the eastern side of the coast, it had one of the finest and most sheltered harbors in the Western Isles. It was a week's journey on foot. Matthew had them take both mules in hopes they could obtain a small cart that they could pull back to The Refuge.

He gave the men a list of supplies and tools to obtain. As he had no money to give them, he told them what places to go to that would credit him for the items being purchased. Many of the supplies and materials consisted of tools, such as a variety of saws, hammers, chisels, augers, as well as a brace and bit, squares and templates, planes and mathematical dividers.

Ideally, he wanted to set up a forge, but that was something that might be obtained, brought in and built later on. He asked the men to get nails of varying diameters and lengths, as well as pegs for joining and securing wood together.

Cloth was a major item, too, and he had a list of clothing materials he wanted them to get as well. Another item he coveted was a spinning wheel and loom, but as with the forge, any cloth making tool that large had to be put on a waiting list.

Matthew asked the men to see if they could get a pair of young oxen. If so, they could have them pull another cart loaded with agricultural items and tools. A plough was needed to help plant more crops. The oxen were a key factor in helping this aspect of expansion as they also could help pull stubborn tree stumps from the ground.

One of the most critical tasks for these men to do was similar to the one given those going to the nearby priory and monastery. He wanted them to tell the townspeople about what he called was "The Story of The Refuge". He asked them to pick the best two storytellers among them who were healthy enough to withstand the rigors such a trip would bring them.

Colin and Terric were chosen.

"If you can bring people back with you, including families, it would be even more of a blessing. It would help show us that we have indeed set our eyes, hearts and feet on God's path and that his hand and honor are upon us."

William cautioned Matthew about making such grand plans to develop The Refuge to the lofty degree he was considering. Langley was worried about the strange events and experiences sustained by the eleven men exposed to the lake in the fen. He thought they were too close and exposed to any other events that might overwhelm them at the cabin from the unearthly place.

Matthew eased the lead tracker's concerns by saying, "You are wise to be cautious, William. When I first arrived here as a young man, the fen was quite active and a place to be avoided. Yet, early on, I put powerful wards, interlaced with much prayer, blessing and the anointing of God onto this whole area of land around us, including The Refuge itself. None of them, or this sacred space, was ever broken or violated. I do not think we have cause to see any harm occur here by such ill power. Truthfully, I believe that even greater mercy and power are extended to us from the nine gifts given to us by the three kings."

The hermit's words soothed Langley's fears. Nevertheless, as the other trackers became well, they set a watch on the camp, dividing the responsibility of doing so between them.

Deep within his heart, Matthew hoped that the three men being sent to Trabaile would prosper in their mission in going there. As they were leaving, he told them to wait up to another five to seven days for anyone wanting to return with them, especially if they were tradesmen, farmers, or involved in other important crafts and skills.

He spent the next month in constant prayer and service to those around him. People began calling him "Grandfather," particularly when the

137

trackers told the others the galvanizing effect his spring water had on them when Scanlan had returned to save them.

People also noticed that the Grandfather was the only one who had a positive effect on Tabard. It was firmly believed that without the hermit's presence near the Captain, the Rover would have weakened and descended into death. Although Tabard did not noticeably improve in his health, his spirit started to become less filled with fear. He would smile when Matthew appeared at his bedside.

The hermit extensively interviewed the trackers and Scanlan about their experiences in getting the Captain. He obtained more information than he thought he originally would when he first began talking with them. He was not so fortunate with Tabard. The man refused to mention anything that occurred to him. Yet, when Matthew questioned Tabard, the old man learned a lot from the Captain's nonverbal responses. Greatworth sensed, knew, that the fen had been revisited by its former inhabitants of old.

Nonetheless, five weeks uneventfully passed in peace. Many at The Refuge accepted this time as a matter of course. Tabard, had he known such time had gone by, would have been filled with a deep concern for their safety.

The Grandfather thought it another series of miracles brought them from God. First, Tabard survived. Second, that he slightly improved. Third, despite the Captain's fear of an attack during the time of his recovery, neither was one made nor were there any further signs that the fen had been occupied at all by friend or foe.

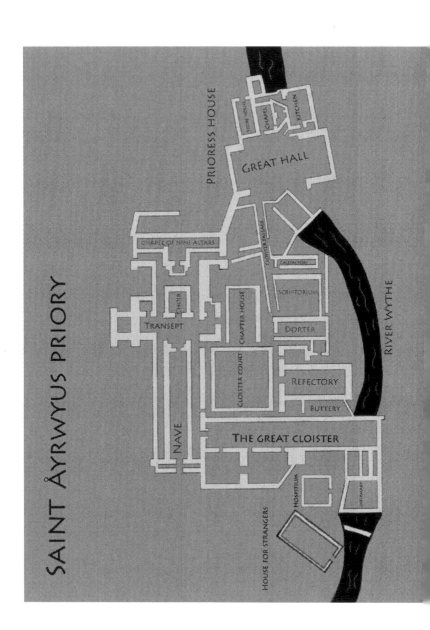

SAINT ÅYRWYUS PRIORY

PRIORESS HOUSE

GREAT HALL

STORE HOUSE

CHAPEL

KITCHEN

CHAPEL OF NINE ALTARS

CLOISTER PASSAGE

CALEFACTORY

SCRIPTORIUM

QUIRE

TRANSEPT

CHAPTER HOUSE

DORTER

CLOISTER COURT

REFECTORY

NAVE

BUTTERY

THE GREAT CLOISTER

RIVER WYTHE

HOSPITIUM

INFIRMARY

HOUSE FOR STRANGERS

CHAPTER SIXTEEN

Evangel felt like she was drowning. She had been so immersed in pursuing spiritual matters she simply ignored everything else in her life. Everything was centered upon the miraculous events with the Rovers, the wolves and now with Tabard. His double mindedness, plus her own, seemed to be suffocating her.

Doubt and serious, critical observation began to invade her understanding of the world that she had learned and acquired at The Refuge since she first was brought here by Matthew. Perhaps this battle over her sense of being was an overflow of the conflict faced by the Captain and his trackers in the fen.

Many times during the day she would get angry.

Perhaps foolish and petulant, too, she thought.

But there was no Scanlan to rescue her from the predations of ambiguity and confusion as he had done so with his fellow Rovers. Carrying this thought further, she knew (as Scanlan had done to help keep the trackers on course in finding Tabard) that she had to tie herself down to something worthwhile to keep her bearings. She clung to the One who had ascended. Often, more than ever before, however, her grip on her former, rock solid faith seemed to slip, and she felt He was gone from her sense of awareness of Him.

She became fearful. She began staying by herself. She took advantage of every opportunity she could take to being alone. Being the only woman at The Refuge made it worse for her. What with Matthew's greater roles of leader, advisor and spiritual shepherd absorbing most of his time and energy, all of these factors helped push her loneliness into becoming even more of an anguish to her.

Less than a week after the tracking parties had returned, Evangel was so fretful and out of sorts with herself that Matthew stopped just taking notice of her misery. Worried about her ever greater reticence around him he decided to say something to her after their dinner. When the supper meal was finished he asked her, "How was your day today?"

Evangel looked at her grandfather. As was her wont, she gave no segue or introduction to her response to him, "I have not been a nice person, lately."

"Why do you say that, Evangel?"

She looked out through the open window, the shutters being thrown completely aside to let the last of the day's light into the great room. Her thoughts were set adrift on the sounds of the evening.

Matthew waited for her to collect her thoughts.

"The day Scanlan and the trackers brought back the Captain, I told him that it was I who failed him."

She paused again and became quiet. She looked at the open door. Her eyes became distant.

Evangel smiled, "Grandfather, you always know when not to say anything to me."

Matthew arose from the table and went to get a fresh pitcher of water. As he passed her, he patted his hand on her shoulder. When he returned, he refilled their cups. "When would you like to visit the priory?"

She laughed. "I would like to see Muriel and Juliana."

The old man greeted this statement with a cautionary one in return. "If you feel somehow responsible for the fate of Captain Tabard, will the weight of that guilt make it difficult to be with the sisters and people at the priory?"

She looked at him quizzically.

"If you are deeply troubled with God right now, Evangel, how will you withstand the questions and scrutiny of the people at the priory?"

"Maybe, it would help me grow stronger, instead," she offered weakly.

143

Matthew sighed and declared, "I think a change of what you see out of that door and this window would be good for you. Early tomorrow morning, I'm going to ask William to take charge of things here for several days. Scanlan and I will accompany you to the priory."

Evangel was surprised at this plan, especially because she thought her grandfather was reveling in his newfound roles.

Before asking him if he was sure he wanted to be away from The Refuge, Matthew said, "What, don't you think my faith, as well as yours, gets set back off its legs when such trouble like this appears?"

When the next morning came, Matthew was up before daylight. He had talked with William and Óengus about his plans, which were quickly set in motion. Three hours after he had gotten up for the day, the hermit headed out on the path to the priory. He and Scanlan carried the heavier packs, much to the protest of Evangel, who said that she could carry her own weight.

Scanlan took one look at her after she made that comment and smiled.

Evangel turned around abruptly and ignored both men. Her thoughts, however, felt brighter to her since she had first stepped onto the trail.

I did not know how much I wanted to leave this place, she said to herself.

As the miles dropped away from the solid pace they kept, both men saw her getting back to her former confident and optimistic self.

Matthew started whistling a tune, and Scanlan sang along with it.

"Once there was a duck from Instance
Who flew forever towards Distance.
His wings were red, his head was brown,
I think it a coincidence.

"The duck flew down, his tail flew up
It caused him to have a big hiccup
His feathers fell out and went to town
Where I got to wear my eider down."

"That is absolutely the worst song I have ever heard sung, Óengus!" she laughed.

"See if ya can go one better, lass," he laughed back at her.

The rest of the hour saw, and heard, out of tune singing and artless lyrics composed on the spot.

It was about noon when Matthew decided to break for a rest.

Evangel asked if they could proceed a bit farther down the path before doing so.

"Are you that eager to get there, Evangel?" Matthew asked.

"Yes, I am, Grandfather, but I would not like to stop here because of the sad memory this place gives me."

She explained to both men that the last time she reached this part of the trail she had taken a break here as well. "I was supposed to meet Muriel and Juliana halfway between The Refuge and the priory, which is on the path further up. I had been walking along steadily for a long time from The Refuge. I sat down and must have been tired because I slept longer than I ever wanted to."

"That doesn't sound so bad," Scanlan proffered.

"No, Óengus, it doesn't," she answered. "The little ones, the wolves, were with me then. We hurried down the trail to greet the sisters...."

Evangel did not complete her thought. Her mind raced ahead of her statement. She became quiet and almost melancholy.

"I understand," said Matthew with compassion, "that's the day when you came back with them and I was being tortured. You've seen and been through many changes and wonderful events that very few people ever witness, Evangel. I'm not trying to make light of what you're feeling, but look at the changes in people and how their lives have been so transformed, including our own."

Scanlan stood looking at her with deference. He said, "If you had not had the love of the Risen One in your heart the way it has been given you, I would not be here singing awful songs."

She smiled wanly at his attempt at humor. Despite her best efforts to prevent them, tears started forming in her eyes. "Thanks, Óengus. It's just that I miss my four–footed companions. And, I don't know where they went and if I will ever see them again. Even if I did, they would never be the same."

Matthew looked at her, reached over and kissed her on her forehead.

"I know, Grandfather, nothing stays the same, right?"

"Not in this transient world, child. Yet, there are many things that remain constant if we can stay within the eternity of God's love."

"I don't know, it just sounds like a saying. If God's love is there, and I have not moved from it, why did he not answer my prayers for Tabard to be unharmed and himself when the trackers brought him back to us?"

The hermit paused to consider her question. "It could be," he continued, "that while the Captain was hurt, he is who he is supposed to be."

"Oh, that's not right. It doesn't make any sense," she complained irritably.

"Perhaps not now to us, but I think there are many forces at play here. Your prayers may have saved him from an even greater plight had he continued on the soul's journey he was electing to take."

A mourning dove sounded its lament in a tree nearby. Another one called back to it behind them.

No one said anything for a while.

"It's all right, Grandfather. Let's stop here and rest. I'm sure we could all use it."

Both men smiled at her. Matthew and Scanlan took off their packs and rested them on the ground. Evangel took her pack off likewise. They divided equal portions of jerky and dried fruit for their noon meal between them.

Scanlan took his water pouch and said, "Great food, excellent company and now water blessed by the Hermit of The Refuge, you cannot go wrong with that now, can you, Evangel?"

She smiled at his efforts to cheer her up. "I can see in you even now how you were able to rescue Tabard and the nine trackers."

148

It was Scanlan's turn to become pensive. He held the water pouch out to her without saying anything.

She took the water and drank from it, passing it over to Matthew when she was done.

As Matthew was drinking, Scanlan was thinking with great effort. They watched him looking at the ground, looking back at them and then listening to the mourning doves calling to one another. Finally, he said, "If I were to say anything about the good and evil I have been exposed to during this last month, I can say with a certainty that if I had not been healed by the power of your prayer, if I had not been filled with the spirit of truth like I was, I could never have done what I did in getting the Captain and the trackers back. I have never done anything like that in my life."

"What are you saying, Óengus?" she queried him.

"It's just that you have angels around you ... we all do ... who help us. They are there because of the love given to us by God. I'm not a cleric or a monk. So, it's difficult for me to explain. Just please don't be so mad with yourself. Maybe you're so close to Him you can't even see it right now."

"Okay, Óengus; thanks for the rope," she said with a small smile accompanying her words. "I must be in my own battle with my doubts and they have overtaken me."

They rested a bit more, and then resumed their walk to the priory. When they had shouldered their packs and started moving out, the mourning dove near them flew overhead. Its wings made a whistling sound as it wound its way over to another nearby tree.

———————⊹—————

They were within reach of St. Åyrwyus Priory, Evangel knew, when the path they were on joined up with the main road. This road headed almost due southwest. The land around them had opened up gradually. The forest was left behind, although there were still substantial tracts of woodland present.

Always before, when she had reached this spot on the road, she looked forward to being at the priory. There was so much to see and do there.

It's not just the difference between living at home in the woods and visiting this beautiful place so filled with things to do and people to see. It's the number of workers here who all contribute to making the priory work together so well. It has so many different parts and places, its buildings and lands are so astonishing, and on such a large scale—I wonder how any one person can make sense of it. It's amazing what they accomplish and get done.

To Evangel, it was exciting to be here, to take in all of the sights, sounds, smells and spiritual splendor that made it such an incredible place whose main purpose was to serve God.

However, today she had terrible misgivings about being here. Life had lost its simplicity. Everywhere she looked now things were so complicated.

Everything seems to exist just fine on its own, she reflected to herself. *Having to think about whether or not there was a higher power was tough enough to consider, but to think that He or She or It answers prayers by insignificant people like me seems, well, farfetched.*

For example, the priory existed financially not only by its patrons providing grants of land to help increase its holdings, but it used these parcels as agricultural means of supporting itself. It functioned like any other well–endowed, and profitably run, manor.

Sheep, cattle, cows, goats, pigs, chickens and geese were raised and used to help provide meat and dairy products for those living there.

151

Farming was essential as well for subsistence, but
also for selling the produce at the market nearby
the priory itself. Horses, mules and oxen helped
provide labor in making it possible to have such
an abundance of crops, in the good seasons, and
to survive in the lean ones.

Wheat was the most prized crop, but other cereal
grains were grown, too, such as barley, oats and rye.
Other vital field crops consisted, for example, of
beans, lentils, peas, cauliflower, cabbage, lettuce, kale
and vetch. Flax was planted, grown and harvested
and was used for fiber in making linen cloth.

Grapes were grown and seriously cultivated
in several large vineyards, as they helped
produce white and red wines that made the
priory a famous winery throughout this part of
the Western Isles.

There were many gardens and their produce
added substantial nutrition to their normal diet.
Carrots, beets, parsnips, turnips, cabbage, onions
and garlic were grown. An ample and diverse
supply of herbs were also raised not only for their
flavoring and nutritional uses, but for their
medicinal purposes, too.

An extensive and sophisticated system of
watering was put into play. A small river actually ran
under part of the priory. Farther downstream, a mill
had been built in order to produce the sisters' own

flour. This flour was also highly prized and sold at market for excellent prices that further benefited the priory's coffers.

The irrigation employed helped water an extensive series of orchards that were surrounded by stone walls, hedges and in two places, moats. Peaches, apples, pears, cherries and medlar were grown. To help aid in pollination, many thousands of bees living in hundreds of beehives were kept for just that purpose. At harvest time, the fruits would be used for drying, for making jams and preserves, and for creating a variety of drinks. Cider, of course, was made from apples, but so was verjuice, a liquid similar to vinegar, which was made from the cider and used in cooking. Perry was made from pears. Ebulon was made from elderberries.

The priory made a variety of spiced or mulled wines. These drinks were used to clear the palate after meals were eaten. Claret was one that Muriel liked. The priory used white wine to make it and it was flavored with a special blend of ginger, mace, nutmeg, cloves, pepper, caraway and other spices, whose names Evangel could never obtain because of the secrecy employed in making the recipe for it.

Matthew loved the priory's ypocras. She knew that it was a spiced wine that could be served hot.

He preferred it made from red wine. It was made from a variety of spices, such as clove, cardamom, cinnamon, ginger, long pepper, grains of paradise and nutmeg or galingale. There were two varieties of it, one consisting of honey, the other of sugar. The ypocras made with sugar was reserved for special guests and those of noble birth. Evangel also knew that her grandfather would occasionally—that is, more often than not—add some of the abbey's brandy to it; or more preferably, follow it up with a small draft by itself.

All of just these interworking parts, specialties, trades, crafts, labor, and layers of people in their different stations in life were *baffling enough to deal with in trying to understand why so many people worshipped something that they could not see*, she thought to herself.

She steeled herself for the moment when she would see the place for the first time on this trip. If everything she just thought of about this place was difficult enough to think about, the buildings of the priory and grounds surrounding it were even more challenging to consider. She held off thinking about such things and listened, instead, to the conversation Matthew and Óengus were having with one another. While listening to them, she felt the initial pangs of the oncoming battle she was to have with other people.

"I would like to make a small, stone chapel in the area of The Refuge," Matthew reflected out loud to Scanlan. "But we need men who are knowledgeable in using stone for such a purpose. We need so much that goes with building such an edifice that we just don't have. I must be deep in one of my dreaming phases."

"I think that's a wonderful idea, Matthew!" Scanlan said with hearty approval. "I think you could dedicate it to the Risen One and it would be a great testament to what He has done for us."

"It's not just what He's done for us alone, Óengus; for He is constant and will supply our every spiritual need. I just am impatient, I guess, and do not see how, what, when, and who will be helping us accomplish such a task. The only thing I know is the where, which is at The Refuge. It is a humbling experience to see a vision when everything around you does not lay claim to what I know will happen."

It was at that moment in their conversation that they reached the top of a rise in the road and looked down the other side and over at the priory in the middle of a verdant valley floor.

Mathew murmured, "Ahhh, at last my eyes can rest on the beautiful St. Åyrwyus Priory."

Scanlan, seeing it for the first time, stopped and soaked in the view.

The priory itself sat on the most arable land in this part of the country. Crops raised there thrived abundantly. Consisting of loam soil, it drained excellently and was easily worked. Those working throughout the priory grounds felt blessed to be in the midst of such bounty.

For miles around, open farmland, orchards, grazing fields and wood stands spread out in beautiful patterns before them. The late afternoon sun was shining on this panorama. Its rays contributed in highlighting the stone buildings to great effect.

The hermit, seeing how the view appealed so to Scanlan, explained some of the key features that they were taking in before them.

"Below us is the Vale of Naomhin. The River Wythe runs through it as you can see. Long ago, the builders of St. Åyrwyus decided that they would have a portion of the priory constructed atop the river. It truly is more of a stream at the point it runs underneath the cloister passage leading to the Great Hall, which is on the eastern side of the complex. When high water occurs, there is little flooding because of the way the architect had his masons and carpenters recreate the riverbed and place thick stone walls on its banks. It seems to help the water pass through without any undue harm.

If a great storm occurs, or if there is an unusual amount of snow melt in the mountains around us to the south, a series of canals were built upriver to help divert the flow of water going downstream. There are vast areas of land that can take this spillage and hold it for future uses. Also, three fairly substantial, moving barriers were built that can be moved into the river itself to help divert the water into three of the largest canals. They are hidden from plain view. It takes a trained eye to find where they are located. As you can also see, the River Wythe serves as part of the defenses of the priory in case it is attacked."

"What about the buildings themselves, Matthew, can you tell me what I'm lookin at from here?" Scanlan asked.

"Surely," Greatworth immediately replied, "the furthest wing of the priory to the east, on the far side of the Great Hall, houses the prioress, Sister Marta Matasan. She has her own chapel, kitchen, and storehouse. Her sleeping quarters arc next to the chapel.

"If you walk back towards us through the cloister passage, to the west, you will pass courtyards and gardens for meditation. Going straight on this passageway, you pass more openings on your left to more gardens. A smaller, but very beautifully arched cloister on the right side, leads you to the Chapel of Nine Altars that is part of the church itself, which is on the north side.

"Yet, if you continue walking straight through the priory, on your left you will pass a small refectory, or dining room, called the Frater House, a large storeroom for grain and similar foodstuffs, the Great Refectory Hall and then the Buttery, which houses the beverages for which the priory is famous.

"The Great Cloister is next and you can observe that it runs north and south to us. The northern part of the cloister brings you to the nave of the Great Church. The five–story tower is facing us on the west.

"In the center is the Great Court, having cloistered walkways surrounding it. Due east of this area is the Chapter House where the sisters daily meet to listen to a chapter of their monastic rule read to them. Their duties are also assigned them for the day. Between the Chapter House and the Great Church is the Dorter, or dormitories, where the sisters sleep."

"Thanks for the tour, Matthew!" Scanlan said.

Matthew started to head down the rise. He noticed that Evangel had not moved. "What is it dear one that I have missed?" he asked her.

She smiled at him saying, "I know that the Scriptorium, where the sisters illuminate or copy manuscripts, is next to the Dorter. And, the Warming House is next to it on the eastern side. It is the only room in the priory proper, besides the kitchen, where a fire is permitted. I think it is also called a Calefactory.

"Also, the buildings separate from the priory and in the foreground facing us, house the quarters for strangers, the Hospitum, which is for distinguished guests, and the infirmary. These three places are allowed to have fires lit in each of their hearths."

"Thank you, Evangel, for your excellent information. Well, Óengus, there you have it: a very brief tour of the place. It took just over a hundred years for the priory to get to this point of practicality, elegance and service to God. When we arrive there, I am sure Prioress Matasan will give us a better tour. I think you will marvel at the craftsmanship displayed in the construction of St. Åyrwyus. The stained glass in the west window of the Great Chapel, and throughout the priory, is stunningly beautiful."

They continued walking toward the priory. When they were several hundred yards from the southeastern side of the buildings, Evangel abruptly stopped walking. She stared at the buildings and then dropped her eyes onto the road in front of her. "Let's go back home, Grandfather. I made a mistake; I don't want to be here at all."

"Evangel, it will be okay," Matthew said consolingly.

She looked up at him with complete defeat written upon her features.

"Well, it probably won't be okay. Most likely the walls will fall down when you walk through the main gate to see the prioress," Matthew jokingly challenged her.

The briefest of smiles crossed her face. She piteously declared, "What can I say to these people who live in such a place of splendor that will sway them to what the Lord has called me to tell them?"

Matthew paused to consider what to answer in response to her question. After holding back his thoughts for a bit, he said, "Maybe it's not up to the likes of you, Óengus and me to worry what God is going to do, or not going to do. He can take care of Himself just fine. You know what you saw, felt and went through. All you have to do is share that with them. God will do the rest. And they will do what's in their hearts."

The young woman shook her head negatively, but remained quiet.

Scanlan jumped right in and unequivocally stated, "Look, lass, you know what they say, 'You can lead a jackass to water but they're the ones that have to drink it.' Maybe God is usin you to bring them to water. Don't let their stubbornness and doubts affect you as well."

"Okay, okay. Both of you have not convinced me at all with your patronage of me. It's too late in the day to turn around and go home. And, I don't think Grandfather would be comfortable sleeping on the ground on the side of the pathway home. Let's get this over and done with!"

They headed to the main gate on the east side of the priory. They crossed over the River Wythe to get to it.

Scanlan knocked on the door and rang the bell to hail the door guard. When he appeared, Matthew introduced himself and his two traveling companions to him. The guard closed the main door and went back inside to give the message that three visitors had arrived. Soon, two sisters came to the door and let them inside.

Suddenly, Evangel realized, they were inside the hallowed grounds.

She whispered to Matthew, "Maybe I can just have a visit with Muriel and Juliana and we can go home tomorrow."

Matthew put a finger up to his lips to indicate she should not be saying anything within the sisters' hearing.

161

They were led along the cloister passage to a visitors' room adjoining the Great Hall. As Matthew had predicted, Scanlan was having great difficulty following the sisters. The beauty of the place began mesmerizing Óengus from the moment he set foot within the priory. He kept stopping, or wanting to stop, in order to admire the elegance and unique construction of everything surrounding him.

Matthew apologized to the sisters, saying, "You must forgive Master Scanlan for his waywardness in following you. He is looking at this beautiful place for the very first time."

"We understand Brother Greatworth. His is not an unusual response to being in the priory. Many of us who have been here for a while still feel the same way."

The sisters brought them to the visitors' room and left them there, where they waited another half an hour for someone else to acknowledge their presence.

When someone, whom Matthew had never seen before, did come to greet them, it was done so with all the earmarks of discourtesy. The prioress did not see them. They were told that she was out on the priory grounds overseeing work being done in the orchards.

The hermit thought the likelihood of Sister Marta Matasan doing something that strenuous was doubtful. She was known more for her being sedentary than active.

The prowess of this prioress is proven in her poverty of spirit.

He smiled inside himself at his attempt at alliterative sarcasm. Yet, his internal levity masked his concern over the way they were being ignored and treated so brusquely.

As the sister who had addressed them was leaving the room, Matthew stated, "In all my years of being here, doing errands for the priory and seeing to their wellbeing with the abbot at Dawn's Abby, I have never been greeted so…" he searched for the right word and found it: "effusively."

The woman paused in her autocratic walk out of the room. She turned and looked over the heads at the three of them.

Matthew took advantage of her somewhat undivided attention. "I would like to know your name as I think introductions are part of a civil and social code this priory has always followed. I would also like to know if and when Prioress Matasan will see us. Finally, I do not think we should be staying here in this luxurious room for the rest of the evening. Do you not think it fit that we are granted the mercy extended to pilgrims and travelers in this realm? That we are in need of refreshing ourselves and having a place to retire for the evening?"

The woman looked at them as though they were not in the room with her. In a voice dripping with impatience at having to deal with them she said, "I am neither at your disposal at this time, nor am I inclined to have you here at all on our fair grounds. You can either wait here for our decision on what to do with you, or you can leave and go back to that deluge of yours."

Neither saying another word nor looking over their heads anymore, she left the room.

"Well, Grandfather, she was rude!" exclaimed Evangel.

Scanlan shook his head in disbelief. "She referred to this place as being on fair grounds. Sounds as though we're at a tourney!"

"I think we'll go out of the priory proper and visit the groundskeeper's quarters where he does his business for the priory," Matthew stated flatly. "He's an old friend of mine and owes me many favors over the years. I was the one who helped him obtain his present job."

All three stood up from the chairs in which they had been seated and left the room. No one escorted them from the visitors' chamber in which they had so patiently waited. They let themselves out through the same door where they had first entered the priory.

Walking back across the bridge over the River Wythe, Matthew said aloud, "Not a propitious moment for us back there, wouldn't you say?" then laughed.

Evangel and Scanlan looked at him as if he had gone daft.

The hermit not only kept laughing, but also roared in approval. "Don't you see," he crowed, "if the Hand of God was not upon us, they would have been polite, charming and beyond hospitable to us. Something's got them frightened. What do you think that is, eh?!"

"Why you old fox," remonstrated Scanlan, "you planned it that way, didn't you!"

The hermit grinned back at him.

Evangel was deep in thought. The two men left her in peace to work out whatever was in her heart and mind.

It was almost dark out. Matthew led them to the groundskeeper's quarters from which the man worked during the day. The large building the hermit brought them to was made of crafted stone. It was renowned for its natural light gray luster, which was highlighted by a rich combination of salt and pepper speckles that seemed to glow throughout the granite.

Small flecks of mica picked up the last of the sunlight and scattered its reflection into their eyes.

Matthew knocked on the sturdily built, front wooden door with his staff.

A gruff voice, in words sounding as though they were being dragged through watery gravel, declared, "Who's there, don't ya know!"

"Well now, Master Groundskeeper, has the world become such that you just growl and snarl even at pilgrims on your very doorstep?" Matthew answered in a surprisingly similar voice as the one they were hearing from inside the building.

The door was recklessly thrown wide open. Standing there was a tall rotund man, grinning as though he was the most jovial man in the world. "Is that a fact, Master Hermit, don't ya know!"

The man stepped out of his quarters and onto the path where they were gathered around the entrance to his business. He went halfway out to the road going by his office, where he stopped and looked left and right, as well as outwards into the gathering gloom.

On his way back down the path to where they were standing waiting for him, he bluntly asserted, "Desperate times make for desperate people and desperate measures, my friend. Come in, come in: don't just stand here on ceremony and your forest politeness."

The groundskeeper ushered them through the door with what Evangel thought *seems like too much ceremony.*

166

Entering the building with his guests crowded around him, and with the front door still wide open, he asked them, "So, how far has it taken you to be here finally at this door?"

This question just did not seem to make any sense to either Evangel or Scanlan.

Not slowing down in his long windedness or nonsensical babbling, he continued peppering them with a series of questions. It was only until after the door was shut by Greatworth and the groundskeeper had brought them into his office, did he ask a final question.

"So my arboreal friend," he said looking at Matthew, "how are you and your companions faring, especially since your visit to the guest chamber next to the Great Hall?"

Not waiting for their reply, he interjected, "I hope well after your daylong trip here from The Refuge."

The groundskeeper went back to the door through which they had just entered. He quietly opened it about the width of one of his large capable hands. This secretive action was in sharp contrast to the outward bluster he had just displayed. Satisfied with his appraisal, he closed his front door gently. He walked back into the center of the room where he helped them take off their packs and traveling cloaks. Once that task was accomplished he bade them to sit down and rest from their travel.

To Scanlan, who was tired from the day's journey, it seemed as though the groundskeeper instantaneously brought them ale and cups. *Soon enough and quicker than thought, he's served us; and, here I am drinkin as though nothin odd ever happened here to us at the priory.*

The two older men talked about the weather, crops, reprised the past winter's harshness, and droned on about bees, honey and taking a tour of the priory. At least that is what Evangel heard them say. Their patter back and forth soon helped put her to sleep.

Scanlan, after the initial surprise of the warmth of the welcome they received, drank several more cups of ale. Soon enough as well, his head fell forward on his chest and he slept. A gentle snoring started accompanying the rise and fall of his steady breathing.

"Now that we got the young ones bored and sleeping," Finley said, "you can stay here in this stone dwelling. It's big enough to house five large families, so there's no problem with a lack of space. Too much house for my liking, anyways."

"Thank you, my brother," replied Matthew.

"It doesn't seem that long ago when you and I were squirts taking our brotherly vows," Finley said with a sigh. "It also seems we did so for far different reasons than many others."

"Yes, we tacked our ships a different way than the rest."

Matthew, upon hearing Finley's last statement, raised his cup of ale to his host and said, "May the Risen One shine on you and yours; may He bless you in all ways, strengthening your needs while glorifying Him."

"I see you still have the gift of words, hermit."

"And you, groundskeeper, I see you still do not lack for astuteness."

Both men laughed.

Scanlan opened his eyes wide and acted as though he was going to stand. Instead, he yawned, stretched and fell into a deeper sleep than the one before from which he had just awoken.

"Is it true what the women were saying when they returned to the priory from your place?" Finley asked.

"Yes," answered Matthew immediately. He paused, thinking about Finley's choice of words. "What do you mean 'were saying'?" he added.

"Muriel and Juliana have been severely sentenced on account of what the Prioress is calling 'wild hysteria and unfounded heresy'."

"What's been done to them, Finley?" the hermit worriedly asked.

"They've been placed in the lowest part of the priory, underneath the buttery. They're not to see the light of day until they recant. They have to apologize to every sister and member of this community in public and to each individual person in private. They're fed once a day, sometimes not. They get a few slices of dried, moldy cheese and inedible bread."

"Knowing their sense of character, honesty and commitment to God," said Matthew, "they'll die down there."

"Aye, hermit, that they will," came the groundskeeper's dour answer.

"Is that the end of it then?"

"No," Finley snorted, "the Prioress and her crew would just get bored seein them take precious time to 'let em sit there till they rot.' Also, it's not Matasan's style."

"Go on, friend, explain," gently ordered Matthew.

"The Prioress has consulted with the Abbot. They decided to nip this rumor these two sisters have growin in the bud. Matasan's called for a trial to be held in the Great Hall the day after tomorrow. Oddly enough, there's to be a big feast the night before, tomorrow eve that is.

"Those of us, like you and me, think the two sisters will be excommunicated and thrown into exile. Other than that prediction, some think the clerics'll just have a mock trial for show. It'll end with Muriel and Juliana bein taken outside in front of the Great Window of the chapel and burned at the stake."

Matthew stood up. His legs were "feeling all pins and needles," he announced. He stamped them loud enough to wake the two who had fallen asleep.

"Well on that note of optimism, I say 'Good Night' to you. Thank you, Finley, for your kindness and mercy in putting us up here."

"You're welcome, don't ya know. Help yerselves to bein at home. You know this place as well as I do."

Finley took a night lantern off of one of the hooks next to the door. Opening the shutter to it, he walked over to a small fire that was ablaze in the hearth. He took a slightly used taper from a small box next to the hearth, got a flame going on its other end and lit the candle already placed in the lantern.

As the groundskeeper made his way out the door, Greatworth said to him, "I expect you'll be here before first light tomorrow morning."

"Be bringin ya somethin ta break yer fast, too, don't ya know!" came the brusque reply.

Greatworth lit three night candles at the hearth. Handing one to Óengus, he gave him verbal instructions for finding a first floor bedroom. Evangel and her grandfather walked up to the second floor. As they started going up the solidly made wooden stairs, he gave her the second lit candle.

"A time of testing has arrived, child," he announced to her. "Even though it may not seem like it to you, it is more for those who presently hold worldly control and power over the meek."

She was too tired to comprehend fully what he was implying to her.

"It's all right, Granddaughter, we'll speak more of this tomorrow."

Matthew showed Evangel to her quarters.

He then went to his own.

In looking through the windows of the stone house from outside, one of the priory guards watched three candles in their own rooms separately go out for the night. He stayed there until daylight.

The three pilgrims inside slept soundly, despite the events about to be experienced by them.

CHAPTER SEVENTEEN

Early morning was ushered in by Finley's arrival at the door to his office. He was accompanied by his wife and two eldest children. They had brought with them food to help the three guests inside break their fast.

Before he could knock at the door, Matthew, who had been up before light, opened it with a great show and good morning hurrah.

"Good morn to you, sir, and Mrs. Finley and your two fine children as well, Abigail and Edward," he said grandly. "Come in; come in. Ahhh, and I see you brought us some of your wonderful victuals for us this morn: splendid!"

"Good morn to you, hermit. And it looks like it will shape up and be fine weather for tendin to the grounds, don't ya know," came Finley's voluble retort.

As Mrs. Finley and her children went into the stone house, both men looked out at the beginning light dawning in the east. Neither one commented to the other about the recently replaced priory guard. He had just started his new shift and was blatantly watching them from across the road.

All of them gathered into a kitchen area where there was a large table filled with all of Finley's implements and paperwork that helped him keep track of the priory's land and buildings.

"Here, here," he said somewhat apologetically, "let's clear some of this stuff out of the way so's you can eat the grand food Mrs. Finley prepared for you. And, I see that your granddaughter is awake and Master Scanlan as well. I trust that you had a restful sleep?"

Both young people replied that they had gotten a good rest. They thanked Finley, his wife and children for their kindness to the three of them.

After serving the food they had brought, Finley's wife and two children left.

At the door ready to go outside, Mrs. Finley smiled warmly and said, "Blessings upon you and yours, Master Hermit." Turning to her husband, she directed him to "be sure you collect our table settings when they're done so we can take care of them at our home, Mr. Finley."

"Yes, dear," he replied. He also went to the door, opened it and loudly declared his love for all those in his family. "Pray, have a day filled with the good Lord's blessings," he said as he ushered them through the doorway out toward the road.

Finley reentered his office, and sat down near the hearth in which Evangel had lit a small fire to take away the damp early morning chill. He patiently waited for them to finish their morning fare.

Once their meal was eaten with great appetite and appreciation, Matthew and Finley made plans for the day. They agreed with one another that staying in Finley's working quarters was the best place for them.

"If they wanted you gone, they would have escorted you off the grounds of the priory," Finley informed them.

The hermit agreed with this observation. "Yes, and I think knowing where we are and what we're doing gives them an opportunity to keep their eye on us. Otherwise, they would've put us under lock and key, don't ya know, eh Finley?"

Finley smiled briefly, having something else he wanted to say. "Today and tomorrow are big events for them. As I said to ya's last eve, there's a banquet feast for the Abbot and special guests tonight. Tomorrow is the trial they're putting up for show against the two sisters."

Evangel, clearly concerned, anxiously asked, "Will they let us near any of these events, Master Finley?"

The groundskeeper scratched his head abstractly and answered, "The banquet tonight in the Great Hall will be filled to overflowing. They will have their hands full setting it all up, welcoming guests, taking care of their needs, and preparing the food itself. This last week, everyone involved in the cooking, cleaning, and care of the place has been beside themselves in getting everything ready. Your attendance at the feast will be noted, but I believe they do not want to make a scene over your being present."

Matthew sagely observed, "No, if we stay the day after, which we should for Muriel and Juliana's sake, I think they will get serious with us. After all, we're the ones the two precious sisters have been talking about that's put them under house arrest."

"I believe, Master Hermit," Finley strongly suggested, "you and the young man here can come and work with me throughout the day when I leave soon to make my rounds." Looking directly at Óengus, Finley said with some irony in his voice, "We'll work you through the bone out there on the grounds. We'll be somewhat easier on the old one, though. I have to make sure he lasts the day so's he can attend tonight's special entertainment."

"What entertainment will that be, sir?" asked Scanlan.

"The priory is all high and mighty over the visit of one of the Western Isles greatest bards, Diarmad Somairhle. If you haven't noticed, we have visitors already flocking here like geese going north for the springtime. Even members of the King's court are already, or soon will be, here. The bard Somairhle's been touched by divinity. At least so it's been told. I don't have any proof such is the case. I'm told he has the sharpest tongue, most dreaded wit and sought-after ability to turn a phrase to praise a king or host. He's got our own rhapsodes, skalds and filidh all up in arms with his prowess, which they are fully jealous of over his giftedness."

"Prioress Matasan must think she's calling down heaven with this artist's gifts," opined Greatworth. "Plus, she gets herself and the priory to be the center of attention for all who are notable and mighty."

"Aye, Master Greatworth," Finley agreed, "She's after more tithes, land and coin be flowin her way. She and the Abbot Ailwin Athdar have been competin against one another for several decades now. It's at its height of rivalry with one another. Each one acts like a powerful overlord, vyin for and controlling estates throughout the realm. Their eyes and stomachs cannot get enough control over the amount of land and resources they ache for every day of their lives."

"Will there be other storytellers playin at this feast, Master Finley?" asked Scanlan, who patiently waited for an opening in Finley's characterization of the two chief clerics in the area.

"Aye, lad, but they're just for packin the stars with more luster for the wealthy and the pride of Sister Matasan. They'll just be watchin the master poet to see if they can pick up secrets of their trade."

"She best be careful," Matthew chuckled, "in having this genius so unleashed within the walls of her domain."

"Why do you say that, Grandfather?" asked Evangel.

"Because this bard and his kind do carry much power in their words. They can soothe men's anger as easily as most drink a cup of ale. Likewise, they can inflame men's passions to incite them into doing anything their artistry deems them to do." Matthew did not add any other explanation to his statement to her.

She looked puzzled and did not quite know what he was implying to her.

Finley, unobserved by Evangel and Óengus, looked at Matthew and winked at him.

The groundskeeper looked at Evangel and said, "I'm goin to send my wife and children here to be with you today while we are out in the fields. There'll be a lot of other women and their children comin by as well to see her, and you. I will be sure to have some of my men nearby. One will have a horse ready to ride to me if needs be. We will have horses near us as well. It won't take us long to get back here at all. Yet, Evangel, I don't think that anyone from the priory will be botherin you."

Evangel thanked him for his foresight and protection.

With the meal and conversation over, the men walked out of the house. Finley gave a boisterous adieu to Evangel. "My wife and children will be with you soon. As a matter of fact, I hear them comin down the road now. You'll be in good hands, lass, don't ya know!"

———————+—

Finley was as good as his word about putting Matthew and Óengus to work on the grounds of the priory. Throughout the time that they were with him, he kept them busy. He took them out to the orchards, to several wood stands and then to the fields where weeding was being done between the rows of crops being grown.

An interesting circumstance started to happen between those working on the land and with Matthew and Óengus. It then repeated itself until it became a ritual for the day.

Finley had Scanlan doing hard physical labor in all of the various places in which he had the young man working. Scanlan worked alongside the men and women in the orchards, woods and fields. He never complained or held back in his energy and dedication in getting the job he was assigned completed to the best of his ability. People around him who were working with him for the first time were skeptical of his ability and strength to get the job done. Once Óengus learned what he was supposed to do, he became a delight to be with for he understood the nature of hard work outdoors. He knew how to make the work, if not easy, tolerable and perhaps even enjoyable.

When the groundskeeper called for a break in the work routine Scanlan was doing, Finley would go and talk with him. First one, then another worker, went over to where the two were standing. Sometimes Finley and the young man would be just talking easily and laughing good naturedly. Other times, they would be taking a drink of water, or also eating a small wedge of cheese and pieces of dried fruit.

The first laborer who came up to Óengus happened to be the overseer for the fruit trees and berry shrubs. He approached Scanlan directly, shaking his hand with great strength. Scanlan easily returned the firmness of the overseer's grip. They eyed one another in the meantime until the overseer said, "My name's Sean. Pleased to meet you, Master Scanlan."

The young man did not register visible surprise that Sean already knew his name. He simply and sincerely said, "Likewise!"

"Is it true," Sean plunged ahead, "that you held down the old man over there while your boss man took out is eyes?"

"Aye, tis a true and fair statement," agreed Óengus.

"And where were the ermit's eyes put once they were taken out of is ead?" he asked with great interest.

"Captain Tabard placed them on a cuttin stump in front of Matthew. He put them in a line like they were a natural pair of eyes lookin back at em."

"'Are them the same eyes he got in his ead now, do you know?" The grower asked with a bit of awe in his voice.

"No," came the answer, "he's got another pair of eyes."

"He does, does e!"

"Aye, Sean. His new pair came from the Lord havin Evangel pray that his sight be restored."

Sean hesitated a bit in asking another question. He then wondered with a bit of dread, "So's your tellin me he sees through God's eyes...."

Scanlan knew that what the man was astonished about made sense. *The hermit does see through the eyes God gave him,* he considered to himself silently.

"Was it the one they say arose that helped the lass do this saintly deed?" the grower asked.

"Aye it was," Scanlan said succinctly. He could see that the grower was struggling with something else that puzzled him.

"Your friends with him and not mortal enemies; ow's that possible?" Sean challenged the young man.

"I thought that, too, Sean, after it first happened in front of our doubtin eyes. But Master Greatworth and me are friends because it wasn't just the eyes of the hermit that were healed. It was also the way we looked at things, too, that was healed."

The grower shook his head in admiration, smiled and shook Scanlan's hand again, even more firmly than at first. "Thank ye, lad. Tis a blessin you just gave me from the Lord...the Risen One, ye say!"

Before walking back to work, Sean firmly slapped the palm of his hand on Scanlan's left shoulder blade. The man walked away talking to himself about what he had just heard.

This type of conversation rapidly started to repeat itself. Soon enough, a line of men, women and children formed to ask, puzzle out with him, express amazement, challenge his veracity, and sometimes invoke a blessing on the young man.

Finley took it all in stride.

Scanlan, by the time he was working on his third assignment, which was at a second stand of trees where wood cutting was being done, started to figure out that the groundskeeper was helping spur this activity on purposefully. Just when the line of people seeing him was the largest, Finley would announce that they had to move on to their next location.

I think Finley knows how to create more interest in our being here, the young man thought. *As a matter of fact, I think he knows a lot more than the way he acts with others outside of his quarters.*

Scanlan, however, was not given much room to ponder over what was happening. There was no time for such reflection to take place.

Matthew had similar experiences with the priory laborers as did Scanlan. Everyone who met with the hermit knew his name and addressed him as Master, or Brother, Greatworth.

Finley had the old man doing minor chores and having him be sure the workers had whatever they needed to work with at all times. Matthew would come up to them on their breaks and serve them their refreshment.

It was an older woman who first approached him. She never even introduced herself to him. Nervous at first, she asked, "Did your daughter pray over your blinded eyes?"

"Well, mum, thank you for asking. God Bless you for your interest in what He has done. My adopted granddaughter, Evangel, prayed that the Risen One would restore my sight in this world. This was done in front of the three great kings who bore testimony of Him to us. Yes, and it was so," he ended gently.

"You see through the eyes God gave you," she stated as a matter of fact.

"Aye, that I do," he said with a smile.

The woman stood in front of him. Silent now, she reached up with her hands and cupped her palms over his eyes. Tears fell from her own.

Similar scenes reoccurred like this one wherever he went with Finlay throughout the day. It reached the point where Matthew did not do any physical work in the fields as Finley said he would be doing for that day.

When the hermit reflected upon this same notion, he laughed and said to himself, *That old rascal knew that I was going to be doing work of a different kind in fields ripe for a spiritual harvest.*

———————————+—»

Evangel started the day helping Mrs. Finley in patching up clothes and also in cleaning up the stone house. However, there were neither many clothes to repair nor much to clean in the house. She ended up sitting with her and listening to her talk about many of the details of all of her daily activities, the children (they had seven), her friends and life at the priory.

Evangel, listening to her prate on about the sicknesses and health of the Finley brood, thought, *How am I going to get through this day? Mrs. Finley is a lovely woman, but why is she going on and on about everything? I wonder if she talks this way all of the time. Wait, her husband does the same thing!*

As soon as she began to have her suspicions about the Finleys, there was a knock on the door. Mrs. Finley shouted at one of her children, "Now go see who that is, will you, lad?"

Evangel thought she saw something like relief on Mrs. Finley's face, that there was the possibility of company to interrupt her soliloquy to Evangel.

When Mrs. Finley's son, *Adam is his name, I think*, opened the front door to see who was knocking at it, Evangel could observe from where she was sitting that there were at least two mothers present with a minimum of a dozen to fifteen children accompanying them.

"Ma!" shouted Adam, "Gisela, Nesta and Emma are here with their brats."

"All right now, Adam," Mrs. Finley responded, "I have eyes in my head. I can see that they're there. Stop yellin and be more polite. Mind yer manners in front of Evangel."

Adam hung his head sheepishly. However, in a flash of inspiration he said eagerly, "There's too many of em to put here in Da's workplace. Maybe we should go in back to the yard where the gardens are!"

"Now that's my boy!" approved Mrs. Finley. She got up, asked Evangel to follow her, and went to the front door to meet with the mothers and their children.

After greetings and introductions were briefly made, Mrs. Finley ordered everyone to follow her around to the other side of the stone house.

"Too many of yehs to handle in Finley's office. So, my boy, Adam here, got it right. We're all goin to the backyard and set in the garden…." she said, seemingly out of breath and walking ahead of them at the same time.

They could barely understand half of what Mrs. Finley was gabbling at them.

She did stop briefly once she was out the front door. She looked across the road at the priory guard standing there watching them. "You can come with us too, Henry Fulk, instead of just standin there n gawkin at us."

The guard ducked his head as though an arrow was shot, or, spear had just been hurled, at him. In a dull, recalcitrant voice he said, "Okay. Good morn to you, Mrs. Finley. Are you leavin yer usband's quarters, now?"

In a louder voice than she was just using, Mrs. Finley told Henry, "We're goin roun back. Yer welcome to join us!"

The guard shook his head as if to say that he was not going with her.

Ignoring his nonverbal response, Mrs. Finley continued talking to everyone and no one in particular. "...Lord knows there's plenty of room. It's pretty there. I think our guest today will like it, too!"

Turning the last corner of the part of the stone house Mrs. Finley was taking them around, Evangel was able to behold a beautifully built, sought-after cloister. The cloister was set around a large flowering and herb garden. Scattered throughout this meditative garden were fruit trees. Apples, pears and cherries were beginning to form on their particular branches.

There were also several pools of water aesthetically located to show off the various types of flowering shrubs and perennials planted abundantly within the cloistered area. One pond had a fountain as well as fish in it. Its plashing sound added to the pleasure of being within the bounds of the garden.

Before the children could break away and run into the garden, their mothers admonished them to be careful where they were going and not to trample any flowers underneath their feet. The older children were assigned to monitoring the younger ones.

When Evangel left the cloistered walkway to enter the garden, she could not but help notice the use of stone to form not only the garden paths themselves, but the patterns she could see set within them also. *It must have taken hours and hours just to find the right stones to make the designs inset within the walks*, she thought.

On parts of the walls inside the cloister, the art of espalier was shown off to beautiful effect. Variegated ivy, climbing vines, and roses, as well as pear and apple trees were used and displayed in a range of geometric patterns. Evangel saw diamonds, rectangles and even a flame arrangement visible to her as everyone walked to the south end of the garden.

Birds flitted among the trees. A wide variety of hummingbirds zipped by her head and chased after one another in competition for nectar and dominance over the other. When she looked over the cloister wall, she could see a mountain range looming off in the distance.

Mrs. Finley was right, she thought, *her guest not only likes it, but has fallen in love with it!*

They walked to where benches and chairs had been thoughtfully arranged so that once seated, viewers could appreciate the various nuances and subtleties of the garden before them.

The women sat down together. Soon all four of them, except for Evangel, were easily talking about matters that most concerned them. The conversation was light, though, and not the way it was when Evangel was with Mrs. Finley in the stone house.

Evangel became lost in the garden's beauty. She watched it change before her eyes as the natural light of the day became stronger.

She suddenly noticed that there was complete quiet, except for the insects and bees, the leaves swaying in the slight breeze that had sprung up and the fountain pearling and murmuring in the background.

"Evangel?" Mrs. Finley asked.

She looked over to her, "Yes?"

"There are children here who would like to see and talk with you," Mrs. Finley announced gently. "Is that okay?"

"Why, of course...." and much to her surprise, Evangel saw all of the children that were at the door of the stone house and who all had gone to play in the garden, were now in a semicircle before her.

What just happened? she wondered. *Did I just fall asleep!*

Mrs. Finley, with great gentleness, picked up one of Evangel's hands and held it in both of hers. "It's just fine, lass," she soothed sincerely. "Everything is good. This garden has the effects your feeling on many folk who enter it, especially for the first time. This is Finley's favorite place to be. He's spent almost half a century making this place like you see it now."

Evangel nodded her head at Mrs. Finley.

One of the younger children walked up to Evangel and tugged her by the hem of the young woman's pale blue, woolen dress.

She looked down at the child seeking her attention.

"Yes, little one?" she asked.

In a small, high voice the little girl queried the young woman, "Are ye the lady who killed a man with yer elbow?"

Evangel did not know at first how best to respond to such a question. While she was thinking how to do so, she heard some of the children snickering in the background.

She looked first at Mrs. Finley, and then at all three mothers. No one cautioned her in responding to the little girl's question. Evangel took a deep breath and said, "Yes I did. He was doing something evil to my grandfather."

"Were you mad?"

"Yes, but mostly terrified!"

"Were the monster ghosts yelling at you!"

"No," little one. There were three small wolves who turned into wind and flames. In each flame, a great king appeared. They spoke of their love of a Risen One and of his love for all of us."

"Oh," came a dissatisfied response.

"The monsters happened to be human, child," she explained.

Another little girl bravely walked up beside the first one. "Is that why you put your elbow in the man's nose, because he was being a monster?"

She shook her head up and down briefly and said, "Yes. But I was angry and very worried about

191

my grandfather, who was being beaten and tortured to death. I didn't want him to suffer."

One of the older boys challenged Evangel's story, "How did you know how to do that?"

"I did not know how, the Lord showed me in the instant I did it. I just knew that if I used the end of my elbow and connected it with his nose that the bone in the nose could go into his head further and stop him from hurting others."

In a softer voice, the boy asked politely, "But why did you pray for his healing?"

"That is a very good question. Afterwards, when it was all over, I asked that to myself as well."

"What did you say back to yourself?" the young boy asked.

"If I had not prayed for his healing, I would still be filled with this wish of death. I would have been filled with an injury you can't see. It's called hate. And, I did not want to end up drowning in it. I thought the best revenge was to put the man in the Risen One's hands. Healing him was the best thing to do. It released me into freedom rather than remaining haunted by the ghost of vengeance for the rest of my days...."

There was silence now that greeted her.

The children gathered around their mothers who, in turn, went up to her. They thanked her. Two mothers had tears in their eyes.

The littlest child walked up to Evangel and asked her, "Can I give you a kiss on your cheek?"

She bent down to receive it.

The child not only kissed her, but threw his arms around her neck, too.

For reasons that none of them could account for, people became filled with joy. Yet, many had tears in their eyes.

"Come on, now, children," Nesta said, "we have to get along with our day. Let the Lady have some peace."

Evangel watched them leave. Many of the children kept looking back her way as they walked out of the garden and into the cloistered walkway.

Her honest and kind response to those around her, laced yet with the strength of her will, formed the basis of a very busy day for Mrs. Finley, her children and Evangel. It seemed that word began to spread that the Lady from the Wood was very young, very kind and very much touched by God. She was also very approachable. These singular traits of character, along with what Muriel and Juliana had said to everyone they could speak with at the priory about what happened at The Refuge, led to a crowd of people showing up at Finley's groundskeeping quarters. Combined with Muriel and Juliana's harsh sentence and treatment by the prioress, interest in Evangel and being near her progressed at an almost alarming rate.

Mrs. Finley put her son Adam in charge of guarding the front door to the stone house. He was responsible for telling all those wanting to see and/or speak with Evangel to go to the gardens in the back of the house.

Adam, at one point after being at the front door for a while, sent one of his brothers over to his mother to inform her that three more priory guards had appeared across the street. Their actions were not as low key as before when one guard had been present to observe Finley and his three visitors. They were in constant communication with one another and looking around them frequently.

A steady stream of people started arriving around noon. The line of people coming to see Evangel grew steadily larger and larger. At midafternoon a veritable swarm of people showed up, many of whom had already seen Evangel, but wanted to see more of her. It was obvious that she had captivated them and fired their imaginations. The young woman's forthright manner in responding to them and the questions they asked her went a long way in convincing them of her truthfulness and depth of faith.

Also, word was going around about people seeing and speaking with Matthew and Óengus. Both men were making an impact upon many people on the grounds of the priory, for good and ill purposes. Word spread to other estates and holdings. Some of the invited and distinguished guests that had already arrived for the evening's banquet went to see what people were talking about so much. As the two men, Greatworth and Scanlan, were not conveniently close by, they went to see Evangel.

When she saw the size of the crowd of people trying to see her, she moved out of the gardens and into an uncultivated field. As the crowd grew greater in size, she walked toward a nearby hill where she planned on talking with them there. She wanted to stand partway up on the hill so that they could see and hear her.

The men Finley left to watch over the women and children grew concerned about what might happen when Evangel directly spoke with everyone present with her in the field. Hearing piecemeal throughout the day so far about the extraordinary events that happened at The Refuge was cause enough for concern. Her shared testimony would be in distinct contradiction to the one the priory and nearby monastery were practicing. These men were concerned that things could get easily beyond their control.

A man was sent on horseback to get Finley back to calm things down.

The three priory guards had been increased to a total of fifteen men. Ten of them accompanied the crowd out onto the field, and then followed it to the side of the hill where Evangel had been headed.

People were demonstrably becoming affected by Evangel's presence. Most were in wonder over what she represented to them. Some were incensed at her "treasonous disposition and heretical gospel". No matter the disposition of the people there with her, a sense of tremendous import and excitement was brewing about her presence amidst them.

Evangel reached the hill and walked halfway up. People followed her and those who could not be immediately next to her, patiently stood below her and farther down in the field as well.

As she was answering their questions and talking with them about her experiences, a dozen more priory guards came marching in, thereby adding to the ten already there.

Twenty–two of them stood in a semi–circle at the far end of the crowd away from Evangel. Almost immediately after their arrival, six knights, riding on their coursers, or on a type of all–purpose warhorse called a rouncey, appeared. In company with them were their men–at–arms, squires and attendants. Some of the invited quests also could be seen at the back edge of the people watching Evangel.

When Finley, Matthew and Óengus rode over on their smaller horses, they were stunned at what they saw. While the size of the crowd, and particularly the kinds of people present were daunting enough to them, something else happened that moved their spirits deeply. Clouds had been gathering all day long and had started obscuring the sun in the early afternoon. They arrived in the field when the light from the sun was blocked by the overcast in the sky.

Yet, when they appeared and started riding over to where people were standing, the clouds dramatically parted a bit. Their breaking open allowed a ray of light to shine on the spot where Evangel and the people stood listening to her. People started praying, talking excitedly and pressing closer to her when this break in the clouds occurred.

The priory guards took this moment as a sign to break up the gathering and to bring Evangel to the priory. They started moving in toward her, knocking people roughly out of the way.

One knight became incensed by this uncalled for maneuver. He stood up in his stirrups and shouted, "What you lot are doing is a craven act of cowardice. I demand you stop and regroup in the line from which you first formed."

The sergeant of the priory guard commanded his men to halt. He turned to the knight on his horse and said, "Good Sir Knight, you have no sway or authority on this ground as it is on clerical and sacred land. What we do here is beyond your trust and your business."

The knight laughed heartily upon hearing this insolent response. Five knights joined their comrade in arms by lining up on both sides of where he stood on his horse. Their men–at–arms moved into three phalanxes and arrayed themselves into a battle line. Their squires and attendants saw to their respective knights needs for weapons.

Just as events were drawing to a dangerous impasse, Finley rode to the edge of the crowd. One of the men walking along with him took his horse by the bridle and steadied the animal. The groundskeeper got off the horse and commandingly walked up to where Evangel was standing.

The sunlight around them turned into a rose color. People's voices became hushed. Several of the horses whickered and grew nervous. A brief shower of rain fell. As Finley approached her side, a primary rainbow appeared behind and above the hill. Everything seemed to come to a stop.

First dragonflies appeared and flew through the people standing there. Children excitedly tried catching them. These insects did not stay long, however. They were rapidly replaced by three different kinds of butterflies. Long–tailed Blues, Continental Swallowtails and Yellow–legged Tortoiseshells flew among them.

The crowd became more entranced when these three sets of butterflies flew up in spirals. They created three separate vortexes that sparkled and scintillated from the sun's light reflecting off their wings.

One older child said loudly enough for everyone to hear him exclaim, "Look, Da, it's the three Kings come to see the Lady!"

One by one, people got down on their knees. Men used to combat and suffering did likewise. All six knights got down onto the ground from their horses and put their hands over their hearts or saluted the three rising whirlwinds filled with what looked like beautifully painted butterflies.

Slowly the spirals disappeared from sight.

Finley said, "We at St. Åyrwyus Priory welcome all of you, don't ya know! May we remind and invite you to the banquet tonight in the Great Hall, and ask that you come and bask in the legendary prowess of the Bard Diarmad Somairhle."

When he finished speaking the rainbow also simultaneously disappeared. People actually sighed at its going away from their view.

"Come, Evangel," urged Finley to the young woman, "let us return to your quarters."

He led her by the hand down the hill. She was joined by Matthew and Óengus. They walked toward the three horses that the men rode in haste over to see her.

The knight who first intervened on her behalf walked over to her. "Lady," he formally addressed her, "it would do me honor for my men and me to escort you and yours to your quarters."

Evangel looked at him steadily and asked, "And whom may I have the honor of addressing me in such a gallant manner?"

The knight bowed deeply to her. "My name is Trevelan du Coeur, Lady."

She curtsied in return.

The knight said, "Evangel Greatworth, also known as Jacquelyn Blessingvale, I am honored, nay blessed, to meet you. Pray thee, will you allow me to accompany you?"

"Yes, Sir Trevelan du Coeur; and, thank you for your courtesy.

The knight ordered his rouncy to be brought over to them. His squire soon had the knight's horse in hand and gave the bridle to Sir Trevelan.

The paladin turned to Greatworth and Scanlan and bade them to help Evangel on his horse. Holding the bridle while they did so, he waited until she was seated aside of the saddle.

"Thank you, Lady, for your generosity and bravery of spirit. The horse you ride upon is called Wyn, or friend, in your language. He has been in many battles and attained much honor for me. Often, he has saved my life for another day. I can see from his look that he is proud to carry you onto the field of your own upcoming battle. May his spirit infuse yours with comfort and aid in the trials of combat ahead of you."

Evangel thanked him for his gallantry and compassion.

The priory guards had become confused with their mission. Some were actually smiling and following the lead party. Others hung back and tried to regroup. The sergeant took his helmet off, scratched his head with a distracted air and looked up towards where the butterflies had gone.

The press of the crowd lessened around her. Yet, everyone went back towards the groundskeeper's place with her. They gave her space in the front of the mass of laborers, tradesmen, farmers, wives and husbands, children, priory guards, soldiers, warriors, knights and squires.

People were marveling over what had happened in the field and on the side of the hill. For many, their mood had transitioned from curiosity, disbelief and doubt, and hopeful expectation to wonder and delight, as well as a hunger for more understanding of the events she experienced and tried explaining to them.

A tall, thin serf hesitantly approached where Evangel was sitting sidesaddle on Wyn. A well–worn, tan blouse was fastened around his waist by a leather belt. Hanging from it on his right was a sheath for his leather purse. Another sheath held a knife, which was on his opposite side. As he walked toward her, his dominant hand was kept on the knife's handle.

When the man was ten feet away from her he stopped. Tension rippled throughout the scene.

Wyn's head went up and down. The courser snorted. His ears tipped up and forward at the laborer.

Evangel smiled.

As soon as she did so, the man in front of her went down on one knee, taking off the coarse, sheepskin cap that he had been wearing.

"My Lady," he said, "forgive me for my being before you like this."

"There is nothing to forgive," she replied. We are all one together on this day in God's field."

The man remained silent.

"How may I be of help to you, friend?" she asked.

"I ...my name is Edward, Lady of the Wood."

"It is an honor to meet you Edward."

"Thank you, Lady, but I take it as a blessing to be here with you and your company."

Evangel smiled again at Edward. "Please," she said, "do not remain kneeling. I am no one of merit, but a simple girl."

He cleared his throat and said, "I have been urged on by my friends to ask you a question that many would like to know. May I do so now?"

"What is it that brings you forward to me in such a manner that you must learn?"

Edward looked at Matthew, saying, "It regards Hermit Greatworth's eyes."

He looked back at Evangel, frowned and said, "This question has vexed many of us here today."

"Pray, Edward, what disturbs you and others so?"

"What happened to the eyes that were taken from him so rudely?"

Upon this question being uttered, a shock went through Matthew's whole body.

Evangel saw her grandfather flinch as though he were in great pain.

She frowned and asked for Sir Trevelan to help her off of Wyn.

The knight, who had been standing next to her, obliged her request.

After she once again stood on her own, she walked over to Edward, who seemed to fold into himself at her approach.

"You ask a question no one of us has considered since the moment my Grandfather's former eyes were taken from him. And now, since hearing it I wonder as well."

She looked at Óengus, who stirred himself into motion as though he had been in a daze. He first placed his hand on Matthew's shoulder then dismounted from his horse and walked over to stand beside Evangel.

"Captain Tabard," he said, "after takin the eyes out of Matthew's head placed them on a choppin block where wood was split for The Refuge. With everything happenin so fast, I never looked to see if they were still on the block."

Scanlan turned to the hermit and asked, "Did you see your old eyes when sight was given you through the new ones?"

"No, I never saw them afterwards. I looked, but they were gone," Matthew answered.

"Perhaps one of our companions took them," Óengus suggested.

Silence overwhelmed them.

The wind ruffled their clothes, the horses' manes, and the pennant that was held in one of Sir Trevelan's men–at–arms hands.

Evangel looked at the serf and softly asked, "What do you think, kind Edward?"

He looked at her and became overwhelmed by emotion. Again he kneeled in front of her. "Perhaps," he said, "the Spirit of God is like the wind here with us now. Unseen, it moves according to His will. Perhaps Brother Matthew's former life was put aside. With his new eyes God shows him the world that the Risen One sees."

The wind stopped. The sunshine shone brightly down upon them. Birdsong could be heard. Children laughing. A horse whickered softly.

Evangel reached toward Edward and silently urged him to his feet once more.

"I believe," she said, "the Risen One in the power of the Spirit you just invoked spoke through you just now."

Tears coursed down Edward's face. "My eyes burn," he said, "but they do not sting."

"As do mine," Matthew added.

Wyn walked gently over to Evangel and pushed slightly against one of her shoulders.

Edward laughed. "My time here with you is over," he said.

"Nay," Evangel responded, "it has just begun."

Óengus helped her back on Wyn. He walked over to where he had left his own horse and then sat astride it.

Sir Trevelan once again went to stand next to Evangel.

People were heard murmuring to one another, talking about what had just happened.

A sense of astonishment fell upon many in the crowd. "Evangel," the knight urged, "let us proceed on to Finley's place."

She nodded her head at him, whereupon he took the reins in his hands and led Wyn forward.

Matthew mutely thought, *of all the people present here with us, not one sister or member of the clergy is in view.*

Arriving at the back of Finley's stone house, Sir Trevelan made sure that the hermit and the Rover helped Evangel down from Wyn. His squire again placed the bridle in his own hands, getting Wyn ready to hand him over to the knight when he was in need of his horse once again. Finley announced, "The banquet formally starts at the beginnin' of the last hour of daylight. I would not compromise anyone here in bein late for this festivity. I urge you all now to go your ways and Mrs. Finley and me hope to see you there anon."

Matthew said softly to Finley, "I do not think our presence at this clerically arranged fete is welcome. We have had neither cordial greetings nor invitation to join this celebration of the priory's arranging."

Sir Trevelan, standing up even straighter than before, told the groundskeeper, "I and my men, my brothers–in–arms and any other person here in my company, who is welcome to be with us, will arrive at your front door, Mr. Finley."

Turning to Evangel, he said with great courtesy, "I will personally escort you and yours to the Great Hall. You are welcome to sit with our contingent. I have been told we have some of the best seating in the hall. If you honor my request for your company this evening in the Great Hall, I guarantee you will be able to have a clear view to watch the bard perform, as well as for the people in attendance to observe you."

"Thank you, Sir Trevelan, once more for not only your deference to me and mine, but also for your insight and invitation to the banquet," she answered.

The knight bowed to her graciously. He smiled and mischievously said, "We will be here at the front door on the hour when the feast is to begin. I believe arriving a bit late, not only makes a statement, but it will focus everyone's attention on you when we appear at their door."

With that last statement made, he and his companions settled themselves on their horses and went down the road toward the priory followed by their squires, attendants and men–at–arms.

Finley thanked everyone in his blustery way for being there and bid them goodbye and Godspeed for the moment.

When everyone had gone away, and Finley, his wife and their children were all in the house with Evangel, Matthew and Óengus, Finley went to the front door again. He opened it wide and took a good look around to his satisfaction. Closing it with a flourish he said, "There's not a priory guard in sight."

Óengus, filled with curiosity over the day's events, questioned away at Finley, Mrs. Finley, Matthew and Evangel. He even directed a few questions to the groundskeeper's son, Adam.

His last question was to Finley and Matthew. "Who again is the knight who was so gallant toward Evangel and us?"

Finley looked over at Matthew; who, in turn, looked at Óengus and replied, "Sir Trevelan du Coeur is from the royal court. He is the High King's Champion."

CHAPTER EIGHTEEN

Mrs. Finley seemed disconcerted. Evangel noticed the older woman's uneasiness when she started pacing back and forth from the general vicinity of the front doorway to the two windows at the front of the stone house that were located on either side of the door. She kept looking at the door as though she expected someone to knock on it at any moment. In going past both windows, she would pause, mutter something incoherent to herself and look at the street in anticipation of seeing someone who was there to visit with her.

As the time approached when Sir Trevelan said he would arrive to bring them to the banquet, her restless vigil at the front end of the house became noticeable to all. Finley finally became concerned enough over his wife's increasing distress that he decided to approach her about it. He waited for her to make a complete round of going from the window, to the door, over to the other window and back to the door.

Just as he said, "Dear..."

A knock was heard at the door.

Mrs. Finley rushed over to it and upon opening it, greeted one of her neighbors who was carrying a bundle of clothing in her arms.

"Constance, why hello! What are you doing here? Why aren't you getting ready to go to the banquet?" Mrs. Finley said breathlessly. "Oh, and I see you have Francis with you as well!"

Constance said something to Mrs. Finley, which could not be understood by those inside the house.

A short interchange of words occurred between the two women with the result that Mrs. Finley, along with the help of her husband, took the items Constance and her daughter Francis had been carrying in their arms.

Smiling broadly, Finley said goodbye to them and walked back with his wife to their guests.

"These are for you, Evangel," Mrs. Finley said as she held out to her a beautiful velvet blue dress, a matching shawl and a pair of fine soft leather shoes.

Evangel, not sure what to make of this gift, responded by saying, "Where did such a dress come from?"

"Constance is in charge of the laundry for the sisters. This dress and shoes, along with the shawl, belongs to a sister who just took her vows. She no longer has any use for them. The sister told Constance she wanted you to have them, especially for tonight."

Evangel thanked Mrs. Finley for explaining where the clothes, shawl and shoes came from, and then, with a touch of wonder, thanked her for making it possible for the young woman to wear them.

Matthew looked over at Finley and told him, "Seems Evangel has some support from one of the sisters."

"You may be surprised, but especially after today's events, she has more support than it may appear on the surface right now," Finley said back to Matthew.

"Evangel, let's retire to your room upstairs, and pray let me attend helping you with your evening's clothes," Mrs. Finley said, while giving a mock bow to her at the same time.

The young woman smiled and returned the older woman's gesture.

As the two women went up the stairs the men looked at one another and laughed.

Óengus said, "Well, I hope they don't mind me wearin these same ole rags I had on all day to this feast."

"I think all those people who saw you, Matthew and the Lady today will be glad to have you there," stated Adam proudly.

Evangel had changed her clothes with Mrs. Finley's help. They had come back downstairs and joined Greatworth and Scanlon, along with the rest of the Finley family. The young woman looked radiant. She received many compliments from the rest of them.

Very soon after she and Mrs. Finley had come downstairs, another knock was heard on the door.

Adam became very excited and shouted at his parents, "Can I go see who it is at the door?!?"

Before they could respond, the boy had run quickly over and opened it. He looked outwards and became very still.

A familiar voice boomed gently over him and through the front door into the room where they had been waiting. "Aye, lad. Quick response with the door. Much appreciated! Tell me now: Is the Lady of the Fields and Forest and her retinue ready to be escorted to the banquet?"

Adam stammered a bit, but quickly regained his youthful composure. "Yes, Sir Trevelan, and she looks beautiful, too!"

Warm, lighthearted laughter sounded outside from those who were standing in the path to the stone house and in the road.

"Aye, a truth that can be seen by all. Pray, lad, tell her that my knights, men–at–arms and companions are here to conduct her to this evening's eminent entertainment."

Without responding to Sir Trevelan's announcement to him, Adam ran inside shouting, "Did you hear! Did you hear? He and his grand company of knights, soldiers and squires are waiting for you Lady. Please come back out with me!"

Adam ran to her and grabbed her hand. As he was about to try to run back outside with her in tow, his mother intervened. "Now, Adam. We've got to honor her and her party. The Finleys, too. Take a deep breath, lad. Let go of Evangel's hand. Go on back out to Sir Trevelan and tell him she will be preceded by Brother Greatworth and Master Scanlan. Me and Mr. Finley will follow her outside: You got all that, son?"

"Yes, Ma, I do. Thank you!"

The boy ran laughing outside the door. He came to a stop before the High King's Champion. Composing himself briefly, he stood straight before him. To the pleasant surprise of everyone there, he made a perfect bow and announced what his mother had told him to say.

Applause broke out among those waiting with the knight and the boy.

When Evangel and her escorts appeared at the door, they were greeted sincerely by those waiting for her.

Again Sir Trevelan insisted on Matthew and Óengus escorting Evangel. He urged them to stand beside her, which they did. Instead of having her on his horse Wyn, there was an elegantly designed pageant wagon there in which she could ride in comfort. The wagon was led by four matched horses that were dapple grey in color.

It was the largest and most beautiful wagon she had ever seen of its kind. Realizing, perhaps for the first time that day what was happening to her, she paused and became hesitant in proceeding further.

Matthew, who had been holding her lightly by her left arm, was ready to help her aboard the wagon. He saw her hesitate as well as the brief look of doubt that went across her expression. Covering her indecision artfully, he said, "Well, Scanlan, lass, take a look at this grand six–wheeled wagon. It's got a pivoting fore–axle that allows it to turn with the horses. We could use it to transport most of what we need to rebuild The Refuge."

"Aye, Master Greatworth," Óengus answered admiringly, "she's the finest wagon I've seen; fittin for the Lady and Mrs. Finley to ride in."

Evangel had recovered her poise and let the two men help her step up onto the wagon. She was followed by Mrs. Finley, who was also helped onto the wagon.

Sir Trevelan turned to the hermit and informed him, "You are welcome to get on board the wagon or ride the steeds you rode on earlier in the day. What is your pleasure?"

Matthew looked at the knight with appreciation for his courtesy. "Thank you, Sir Trevelan, for your providing us with such a fine choice of transport. But I would like to take advantage of your foresight in bringing the horses we rode today back to us. If my decision is mutually agreed upon by my two companions, may we ride them alongside you and your distinguished company?"

The knight smiled easily and answered, "Of course. Your horses are in back of the wagon. There are three squires holding the horses and awaiting you and your companions. As the road is wide enough almost all the way to the priory where we will enter it, I urge you to ride alongside the wagon with me."

As the three men went to get their horses, Mrs. Finley called over to Adam, telling him, "I am proud of you, son. A mother could not be any prouder at this moment than me. Now, you go and take the rest of your brothers and sisters over to Gisela's. She, Nesta, Emma and

Constance's families are goin to the affair for the priory's workers that's been set up on the north side of the Church. Make sure that you all get there in one piece. Mr. Finley and me will be there after the bard sings. You got all that, lad?"

"Yes, Ma, I do," he shouted back with a laugh.

She nodded at him. Evangel saw a tear or two appear in her eyes.

The driver of the pageant wagon waited for Sir Trevelan's order to go. The knight, now on Wyn, rode over to the right side of the vehicle. He indicated to Matthew, as the three men approached the front end of the wagon on their horses, to ride between the knight and the wagon. He asked that Finley and Scanlan attend to the left side.

When everyone was in position, the knight waved his left hand forward and the grand company slowly processed down the road toward the priory. They traveled with light hearts, polite words, and a contentment that accompanies confident and secure people on their way towards an excellent evening with one another.

On the ride over to the priory, Matthew and Sir Trevelan talked about matters of the court. Matthew was surprised to hear about the amount of unrest in many of the coastal and delta areas in the Western Isles due to invasions from the south, east and north sides of the great island chain that constituted this large and diversely shaped archipelago.

"Who are these invaders?" asked Matthew.

"They constitute a polyglot group of raiders, barbarians, pirates, malcontents and genuine trouble makers who want what we have worked so hard to attain, Brother Greatworth."

"How serious is this problem, and how long has it been going on at this level of activity?" were the hermit's two follow–up questions.

"Good questions, my friend," the knight acknowledged. "The raiding at this level is something new that we have not seen here in at least century and a half. We have always had small bands and crews of this ilk assail our shores; but it was done piecemeal and the raiding was widely scattered in seemingly random, unplanned patterns.

"In the last several years, we no longer see such innocuous and relatively modest level of incursions as we experienced in the past. These more recent attacks are quite organized, rapacious and in some cases devastatingly effective. Also, the High King believes, based on information he has obtained, there are other interests conjoined with these assaults."

217

"Are these so–called 'interests' from other realms?"

"Assuredly, yet the King maintains that they are being aided by people within our own borders," Sir Trevelan said in a troubled tone of voice.

"Intrigue," cautioned Matthew, "is ever the twin of duplicity."

"Well stated!" the knight said with gusto while clapping his hand on the side of his leg. Wyn shook his head up and down and then from side to side.

The knight laughed, "Right, old friend?" he said to his horse while patting Wyn on his right shoulder.

"Ah, but let us turn our attention to other, more relaxed, matters for the evening. I, we, that is, are looking very much forward to this evening's most agreeable diversion. Diarmad Somairhle is a star in the firmament of poets, singers, historians and storytellers."

"Can you tell us more about him, Sir Trevelan?" asked Evangel. "I have never heard him perform."

The knight turned to her and kindly said, "You are in for a very rare experience, Lady Evangel. Many say who are far more informed than I on such matters, that a skilled bard like he comes along once every thousand years. Seven generations of his forebears successively held the title of bard. He is the eighth generation and the finest of them all.

"Some consider him a prophet reborn from the days of old when our spiritual understandings were just arising and being established. Many fear his gifts of song and rhetoric. His powers in cursing or blessing those around him are legendary even though he is still relatively young for someone as mature as he is in his profession. The High King thinks so well of him that he has bestowed upon Diarmad some of the richest estates in the land."

The knight paused in his exuberant praise of the bard. "Pray forgive me for my soliloquy, my Lady. In brief, I think you will never forget his performance this evening."

Evangel smiled and said, "Thank you, Sir Knight, for your praise of this poet. I do look forward to being in his presence and listening to him."

Sir Trevelan smiled in return and replied, "Lady, Master Greatworth, we are approaching the priory's northeast side. We do so because of the large concourse that is there before the Church and prioress' quarters. She has assigned our people to this area. We will bring you fairly close to the north side of the Great Hall in the wagon. It will be just a slight walk to the gate that opens to the cloister passage leading into the Hall."

The knight paused in his directions and smiled raffishly, "Besides, I hope to delay our appearance a bit more."

Within a half mile of the church, Evangel could see groups of latecomers approaching the priory as well. She was sure that many others were pouring into the place from the west, south and east as well. When the wagon she and Mrs. Finley were riding in was brought as close as possible to the northeast side of the Great Hall itself, Matthew and Óengus were immediately present to help both women down to the ground.

Those who had been in their procession from Finley's office also were in the midst of getting ready to walk towards the priory. As they made the transition from arriving here to getting ready to approach the hall, Evangel took the opportunity to ask Matthew for a blessing.

The hermit smiled and did so. He bowed his head, closed his eyes and prayed:

"We are but pilgrims walking in the vale of this present hour between reality and the arc of time given to us. Our moments in this world are too few; yet, they can provide treasure as well as trouble to us. As I am a servant of the High Lord, I ask that my words reach the Risen One and form a pleasing petition to His Spirit. My child, may the Lord bless you and keep you; may his glory shine down upon you. May the evening ahead be filled with His radiance and that the knowledge of Him, and those who have chosen to follow Him, be given as a surety to all who ask him for such grace. May His peace forever be in your heart, no matter the treasure or trouble gathering around you or lodging itself in your soul. May you walk through this life, and in this evening, knowing His love for you is infinite."

Much to his surprise, when the hermit opened his eyes, he saw that everyone around him, for as far as he could see, had kneeled on the ground and listened to his blessing.

CHAPTER NINETEEN

When all were ready to go in, Sir Trevelan gathered together his large group of people and they proceeded to the northeast gate of the priory. The wide doors of the entranceway were already open. Some of the same men guarded the doors who were in the field with Evangel earlier in the afternoon. As the knight walked by these soldiers, they stood at attention until he passed by them. When they saw that he was leading a large party of people whose foremost members included Evangel, Matthew, Óengus and the Finleys, their eyes opened wider in surprise.

No guard stopped or interfered with their walking through the priory gates, down the eastern end of the cloister passage and into the north entrance of the Great Hall.

Evangel stepped into the hall holding Matthew by his right arm. She leaned on him slightly so that she could look around her at the enormous space dedicated to this part of the priory. To her left was a raised stone dais upon which was seated Prioress Marta Matasan, Abbot Ailwin Athdar and other members of their respective staffs. Distinguished guests of the clergy from other monasteries and priories were also seated at the large table, which took up almost the full width of the hall. These guests were ranked in ascending order according to their prestige and power on both sides of Prioress Matasan and Abbot Athdar.

As they walked into the hall, a man dressed in formal ministerial looking clothes announced them. He struck the iron shod tip of the large ceremonial staff he was carrying sharply on the stone floor three times. In a powerful voice that carried the length and breadth of the hall, he said, "The honorable and puissant Sir Trevelan du Coeur, His Majesty, the High King Peter Áed Menn Rochtmar's, Champion of the Realm, and his guests."

When the announcer reached his last word, "guests", he barely recovered his poise. He had seen that Evangel was in between the Knight and the hermit. Forgetting to mention aloud the other esteemed members of Sir Trevelan's party, it was a slight miracle that the word "guests" was uttered as well as it came off sounding.

Upon this announcement being made, a silence rippled throughout the hall. People farther on down the length of the great room craned their necks to see this odd pairing of people. Some of those who were at the further end of the hall stood up to attain a better glimpse of the Lady from the Woods and the holy hermit by her side.

Sister Matasan was incensed at this turn of events. She started to get to her feet to protest Evangel's presence. Abbot Athdar, touching her right elbow before she could do so, shook his head slightly, discouraging her from making any comment whatsoever.

Another man, dressed very similar to the announcer, ushered them to their seats, which were to the right of the main table and the closest to the entry where they had just entered the hall. A wooden dais had been built for Sir Trevelan and those with whom he wished to favor this evening by having them seated with him on it. In showing them to their respective tables and seating arrangements, the usher kept running his right hand through his shoulder length hair. Evangel could not tell if the man was performing this gesture because he was nervous in seating her, or if it were one that was just peculiar to his nature.

Due to the fact that the knight had preempted the seating order, Sir Trevelan turned to the usher and said, "Kind Sir, thank you for your seeing us to our places. Forgive my impetuosity in redoing the order of seating members of my party."

The usher smiled, bowed adroitly to the knight, and left them alone to their own devices.

The knight placed Evangel to his left. Matthew and Óengus were on the left of Evangel. On the right of Sir Trevelan ranged his knights and their ladies. The Captain of his men–at–arms was also seated at the knight's table. He was in the last seat to Sir Trevelan's right.

Other tables were placed on the stone floor of the hall in front of them. Seated here also were the remaining members of the knight's contingent.

The rest of the people in the Great Hall stood up and applauded as Sir Trevelan and his party arranged themselves at their assigned places. A loud applause erupted from almost everyone in the great hall.

The guests at the head table reluctantly did as well, while the prioress and abbot remained seated. They neither chose to applaud nor give any sign of recognition to the knight. Their lack of decorum was noted and its pointed insult had everyone there remarking about it to one another as well.

Once she had sat down, Evangel felt in a daze.

The High King's Champion spoke to her softly as he was in the midst of looking over his people and acknowledging the greetings of others to him. "Take your time now, Lady, and look about you. Drink it all in because now that I am here, I can see we do have the best seats in the hall."

Evangel looked across from her to the east side of the hall.

Sir Trevelan pointed out to her that a specially constructed stone dais had been temporarily built for the bard to use for his evening performance. "It was built to Bard Somairhle's specifications."

The elegance and beauty of the hall suddenly overwhelmed her. She saw that beautiful tapestries had been artfully laid down onto the stone platform upon which the bard was to perform. They matched those hanging on both sides of the full length of the hall. Out of the entire grand and courtly scene arrayed before her, Evangel could not fathom the fact that someone would be walking on them. She could not even imagine what their worth might be if they were all added up together.

The knight observed her disquiet and tried to distract her from her increasing distress. He informed her that the simple looking harp, which was placed on the highest part of the dais, was positioned there for the bard to use. "It is his personal harp whose construction is a secret. No sweeter and more powerful one is known to exist in this world," he said with a smile.

The rest of the hall, as far down it as she could clearly see was filled with linen covered tables. All were packed with well clothed people seated at them. She also noticed that drinks had already been served and food was at this moment being brought out for the priory's guests. Those at the head table were already eating.

Food and drink were brought to the knight's table. After the drinks were poured, Sir Trevelan stood up. Gradually, the hall became quiet, especially when they saw the knight standing above them on the wooden dais waiting for their attention.

The knight lifted his cup above him. Everyone stood.

The realm's champion gave a toast, "To His Majesty, the High King Peter Áed Menn Rochtmar: Let us drink to his health and to the continued safety and prosperity of the Realm of the Western Isles which he rules and well serves our people."

After the toast was completed and people drank to it, others followed and were given by the great and humble alike. People drank to salutations for the health of the prioress and abbot; they imbibed over the remembrance of those who had fallen on the fields of war. Several members of the clergy had received recent appointments and these individuals were given congratulatory toasts. Some raised their cups to celebrate best wishes to those who were betrothed to one another, or good wishes to those couples having newborns.

During a brief interim between these liquid lauds, praises and honors, Evangel asked Sir Trevelan, "Tell me Sir Knight, where is the Bard Diarmad Somairhle? Is he here with us in the hall?"

"No, my Lady. People say he never celebrates or eats before one of his performances. He spends the time in meditation, prayer and preparation for what he will be presenting to us this evening," the knight answered. "The bard is ensconced in the guest quarters reserved for royalty here at St. Åyrwyus Priory, for truly he is considered an integral and critical member of the King's inner circle of advisors. The High King also appointed him a Lord of the Realm with a guerdon of coin and estates that is the highest amount ever given an individual by the Crown."

"It is dark out presently. Most of the food has been eaten. Will he know when to start his performance?" she asked.

"Yes he will," he kindly responded. The knight smiled at her and added, "You will soon see. Please forgive my reluctance in answering your questions in this regard. I do not wish to mar or ruin his performance for you by letting you know beforehand his manner of presentation. Do you forgive me?"

"Yes, and pray forgive my deluging you with so many intemperate questions," she said apologetically.

"Lady, you have not been intemperate whatsoever; although, if our cups keep being raised to salute others, we will all be most intemperate, indeed!"

It was at that moment when a man far down the south side of the hall stood up to make his contribution of honor in the evening's drinking ritual. With great exuberance as well as disregard for his own weapon and church property, he rapped the hilt of his dagger on top of the table in front of him until he had everyone's attention.

Seeing that he had done so, he offered his toast. "To the Lady Evangel, who sits at the left side of Sir Trevelan du Coeur: May the Lord forever bless her in bringing His light unto us."

People throughout the Great Hall brought themselves to their feet shouting, stamping their feet and exuberantly drinking their cups in approval to his words.

Prioress Matasan, hearing this toast being made, and ignoring the protest of Abbot Athdar not to do so, rose to her feet. Her face was crimson from anger.

"This is an absolute outrage!" she yelled. "It's bad enough that she and her ilk are in this room, uninvited to this affair and in the presence of those who are her superiors. Guards, put her, her hermit and his young lover under house arrest. Take them to where the sisters Muriel and Juliana are being rightfully imprisoned. Take the groundskeeper and his doxy, too!"

A shock of dismay and surprise rippled throughout the hall. A dozen, fully armed guards appeared from the south and east sides of the great room. As they converged onto Sir Trevelan's table, the knight arose in terrible anger and in full battle mode.

He gave a great rallying cry, "All knights, men–at–arms, and those who are prepared to defend the Lady Evangel Greatworth, hearken to me."

Along with the older veterans of war and the young men of his contingent, threescore men and women rushed over to the knight's table.

The prioress was now standing on her table screaming at the top of her lungs, "If there is resistance to my orders, run the fools through with your swords! Take them outside and shoot them with crossbows through their addled pates for unwarranted trespass on holy grounds."

Sir Trevelan countered her squealed commands by urging on those standing with him, "Pray you, those with weapons keep them sheathed and unused. Let us encircle the Lady Evangel. These feckless guards must then hack us apart to get at her. When their recreant actions become known throughout this land and in the surrounding realms, this priory will become a distant memory. I will personally see to its demise."

The prioress now began unleashing invectives at the knight that burned the ears of even the most combat hardened warrior in the hall. The abbot, along with four other clergy members at the head table, managed to get Sister Matasan down off the table and back into her chair.

Sir Trevelan stated very carefully to those standing with him, "Anyone, guard or individual, so inclined to touch any of my people to get at this Lady, will have not only their weapons stripped from them, but will face the full extent of the High King's wrath. I will personally see to it that exile, if not severe punishment, be meted out to them to the full extent of the King's laws and by my office as the High King's Champion."

It was at that moment that a great bass bell sounded.

Those who had been serving the food and drink to the assembly quickly went around the room extinguishing most of the candles and oil lamps. The four great candelabra hanging from the ceiling were brought down within reach and their candles were snuffed out.

Once again the bell knelled.

The candelabra were raised back into their positions above the banqueters.

Large candles and a variety of oil lamps were brought to the stone dais where the evening's entertainment was to take place.

The priory guards still encircled the knight's head table.

The knight's body of men protecting Evangel remained standing protectively around her.

A third time the bell resounded throughout the room, its peal sending shivers of its vibration reverberating against the ears of all those inside the Great Hall.

Several musicians entered the hall and went directly to their places behind the dais where they took their instruments in hand and stood in position waiting for the bard to appear.

People involuntarily braced themselves for the bell to ring once more, but it remained silent. The last pulse still could be heard echoing from the bell itself.

The Great Hall's announcer strode forth in front of the performing dais. He hit the stone floor with his staff three times. Sparks flew away from the steel tip of the staff as it was sharply struck against the granite.

"On the behalf of Sister Marta Matasan, Prioress of St. Åyrwyus Priory, and on the behalf of Brother Ailwin Athdar, Abbot of Dawn's Abbey, we humbly introduce to you the Ri–Eigeas, the Priméces, the Bard of the Realm of the Western Isles, Filidhe Diarmad Somairhle."

As the announcer turned to walk away, Evangel saw a man in a white robe seemingly appear almost instantaneously in front of the stone dais in the other man's place.

She saw a man who seemed ordinary, even plain, to her. He was in his late thirties or early forties. His russet colored hair was long and straight and reached just below his shoulders. Beginning streaks of white ran through it.

His gaze that first glanced at the ceiling, now descended to the tableau of struggle over at the two head tables. The bard ran his hand through his hair while he stepped up onto the stone dais that had been built for him. As he approached his harp, a series of beats were made on two riddle drums, or primitive looking *bodhráns*, with the use of wooden tippers tapping out a simple duple time rhythm. Smaller bell like sounds were made that ran the range of a pentatonic scale. Their combined percussive sound together made a series of point and counterpoint with one another, weaving into a gradual crescendo of sound and increasing speed.

The bard reached his harp and stood next to it.

233

The music suddenly stopped.
He stood relaxed before them and said,

"Your Graces, High King's Champion,
Guards of St. Åyrwyus Priory, Esteemed
and Welcome Guests:

"Is it not amazing but subtle, forsooth, that
the difference between a tocsin and a toxin
is not found in its pronunciation, but in its
presence. One proclaims death: the other
peals away life. If such is the contrivance of
mortality, why wring out our life's moments
in artifice, chicanery and in artful sophis-
tication over our lusts? These are anon but
death in its final reverberation.

"Do you not think that a touch of tolerance
makes a sharp disparity in the way mercy
is shared between everyone?

"If we fail to show our capacity for charity,
for grace and for making our lives into our
greatest art, we are no different than this
stone floor upon which we stand and hold
forth our follies.

"To cover the beauty of the good God's stone, we use herbs like mint, lavender, marjoram, basil, chamomile, sweet fennel and germander. Are not the fatuity, the foolishness, the farce of our collective fancies the herbs we use to cover the excrement we create everywhere we walk in this great valley of time?"

Where a middle aged man had stood, Evangel now witnessed a being who had begun to make a startling transformation. He was changing into a powerful entity of language and meaning. He was holding up a mirror of words that made her see a reflection of what was, what is and what could be the best in all men and women.

The bard stopped his poetic declamation. He stared at the guards who soon became uncomfortable with his gaze upon them. The sergeant at arms dismissed his men. They turned away from Sir Trevelan's table and walked away into the darkness hovering on the fringes of the great room.

Those still standing in a protective semicircle around Evangel relaxed their vigil and sought their seats. Sir Trevelan remained on his feet until all had returned to their places in the hall. He and the bard remained the only two people standing in the Great Hall.

The knight saluted the poet and sat down.

Somairhle nodded his head and bowed graciously toward him.

Evangel, seeing the ease and grace with which he bowed to Sir Trevelan almost said aloud, *Why, it is the usher who sat us here at these tables arrayed before him!*

The usher, turned now into the performer, sat down at his harp. Before placing it before him, he said:

"A sampling of two fevered conundrums:"

He set the harp against him and played a melody in a minor key. The harp sprang alive in his hands. It seemed to Evangel that it became a beast of prey, a hunted and wounded animal. It wept, laughed, wept again. It strained to tear itself away from the hands and grip of its player. If an instrument could free itself from its musician, this one seemed almost to find that liberty. Instead, it settled down and focused its attention on bringing an ancient power into the hall. The bard shifted the song he was playing into a major key. She thought she saw the harp smile in a sudden running waterfall of notes.

The Ri–Eigeas paused in his musical incantation and pronounced:

"The First,

A Canary's Canard

I know a cleric who
Perceives reality through
A window and yet
Tells me it is only a
Reflection that bounces
Back and forth on a
Mirrored mind."

Again, the harp sprang into a race with the awareness of those listening to it. It ran with them into places of light, freedom and the air of the four seasons. Winter spilled its cold and depths of snow into their imaginations. Spring lit up the hopes of their youth; it reminded every listener about plans made in their innocence, for their best selves to lead lives filled with joy and contentment. Summer came roaring in with its greenness, its humidity and heat, its fecundity and earthiness. Fall fell upon the gathering: leaves dropped around them in the colors of the rainbow's full spectrum. Time leapt away from the Great Hall and was held at bay from returning to them, yet for a while.

The harp glittered. Scintillated. Sparked, seared and singed its notes into their souls.

The Filidhe now, not the man, sang with the harp who began teaching him what to say:

**"*The Second,*
A Prophecy**

Somewhere in the lives of
Fantasy and Legend,
The Masters of Power
Enchanted their people
To exist with their laws.
In the cities, the tiniest
Pieces of truth performed
Their cauldron dances in
Tunnels where strangers
Sleep in one another's arms.

In the villages, people
Jaundiced with lives
Spent in spending more,
Nestle further into wealth,
Sweep away the cares of the day.

Even into a solitary shower
Spraying death's ease
In poetic lathering,
Sophism will towel itself wet
With bloodless lies of deceit.

Apostasy will strut wildly by;
People will be soothed into a
False ecstasy, worshipping
Idols that kiss them with a
    Hypnotic Sting.

The stones bled, the animals solidified;
The stars shone black, the trees whitened;
The enchanted bore suns and waters to
Fill the world and the bastard
             Shadowed
             Reality

Breathed its magic in
    Old–dying–young–aging:
    While the legerdemain of
Birth showed its head of beauty,
And none became…"

The poet, the prophet, the orator, the musician, the magician and, then, just the solitary man, stopped playing. A sustained silence greeted him. He had put people into a place of enchantment. They had been transported into a daze of wonder from what they just heard.

The bodhráns and bells worked their way backwards in contradistinction to how they first started at the beginning of the performance.

The bard lifted his harp away from him and stood up. He swept his hand through his hair and bowed to the people.

The great bass bell tolled for the fourth and final time.

It rang so loudly it shook the plates and cups on the tables of the assembly spread out before the stone dais.

When Evangel recovered from the reverberation of the bell, Diarmad Somairhle, the highest bard in the Western Isles, was nowhere to be seen.

CHAPTER TWENTY

Time crept back into the Great Hall. People gradually returned to their everyday sense of self. Candles and oil lamps, including the four great candelabra suspended from the ceiling, were lighted once again. The Great Hall became as fully illuminated as it was before the bard's performance had begun.

Sir Trevelan was the first to regain his wits about him. He called for his men to escort Evangel and her party from the hall. Encouraging his knights' companions, soldiers, friends, guests and the rest of his party to leave with him all at once, he started exiting from the room.

Before Evangel reached the north end of the hall's entry, Sister Matasan's voice cut through the overall chattering and conversations about the bard's performance that filled the large space in the hall.

"You will not be going anywhere, but where I deem, hermit's heretic," she said to the young woman in an eerily capricious tone of voice. "I told you earlier, before you ruined the Bard Diarmad Somairhle's performance, that you are to be held under priory arrest. That was no idle threat, girl."

Sir Trevelan and three of his knights walked with him over to the head table where the prioress was standing.

Looking down at him imperiously where he stood before her, she said, "You, who think you are protected from the High King because of the position he's been forced upon to give you. Your position is at the end of my holy foot; for you are a ludicrous lickspittle, a false fawner, a syphilitic sycophant. I will have you boot licking my own continually for fortnights beyond your reckoning."

Sir Trevelan smiled up at her, "Why, Prioress Matasan, I believe you have a secret and you wish to share it with me."

The sister looked around her. People were frozen into position, listening with avid interest about what was going to transpire between these two notables. She looked back at the knight who had the audacity to address her in such an uncivil manner.

"I have no secret to share with such as you," she declared with acidic rancor.

"Prioress," the knight addressed her, "you have long wanted a liaison with me so that you had the High King's ear. Your seduction of me this evening, while quite flattering is still unachievable. You're too old and feisty for one, as you say, 'such as me'. Besides, the boots that hold the feet you have are not desired by me. Pray wear them out on some other steed of your choosing."

242

As the prioress started to realize what the knight was saying to her, she flushed a deep red and almost purple color. She became speechless.

Sir Trevelan took her lack of a verbal response to him as a dismissal. He bowed to her deeply. The knight turned back around to his company, smiled at them and indicated with his hands that they were through here. They filed orderly out of the room.

The Prioress in a rage never seen by any of those who knew, or thought they knew her, sat down in her seat. She remained there silent for well over an hour.

Evangel and her companions walked with the knight and his company back to the area where she and Mrs. Finley had alighted from the pageant wagon, and Matthew, Óengus and Finley had dismounted from their horses.

Sir Trevelan said to them, once they all had converged at this location, "I fear for your good health, my Lady, for I believe your safety has been compromised by this evening's more than ample entertainment. Prioress Matasan and the rest of the clergy attending this fete we have just observed have become bitter enemies against you."

Matthew intervened at this point in the knight's concern over Evangel. "I am afraid, Sir Knight, that these people were already and bitterly arrayed against her."

"Yes, Brother Matthew, indeed they were. But they are even more deeply set against you and yours now."

"What do you suggest they do?" Finley asked.

"Sir Trevelan looked at all of them in turn, then said, "It is neither safe for you to stay here on your own nor work your way back to The Refuge. You would be stopped and punished. You certainly would disappear from the sight of chivalrous society. May I recommend a course of action to you, my Lady?"

"Most certainly, Sir Trevelan. I am anxious to hear what you have to suggest to us in our current predicament."

"Thank you for your permission," the knight responded with concern remaining in his voice. "I will have the Captain of my men-at-arms, Captain Conrad Vallans, escort you and your party back to Finley's work quarters. The Captain will be accompanied by twenty of our men. He will post a guard around the stone house throughout the night, which will be maintained as though he were on maneuvers in the field.

"When morning light breaks, I and my men will arrive. We will have sent the rest of our contingent on ahead to where our battalion is encamped. They are staying in the foothills that are to the south of here about five miles away. I have sent a messenger already to bring in three companies by tomorrow morning. They will receive my instructions before I arrive to Finley's quarters. We will proceed from that point depending upon what we face at that time."

Matthew, after taking in the information the knight had just shared with them asked, "To where do we proceed?"

"To the High King's court where you will be given fair and hospitable welcome," replied the knight. Does this plan meet with your approval?"

"It does. However, it also puts us in another conflict," Matthew stated flatly.

"Pray tell me, Brother Matthew, what other conflict is added to the burdens facing you now?"

"For propriety's sake, and for the wellbeing of Evangel, Óengus and I must accompany her wherever she goes; for she is my ward and granddaughter. I am the only family she has left to her in this world. Yet, in being with her, I neglect my responsibilities to my humble hermitage in God's Temple. Also, we have men there and we are seeking to expand our home to accommodate those who wish to live in this sacred place. We have sent people out to share with them the extraordinary events that have happened to us only recently."

Scanlan listened to Matthew explain the hermit's concern for Evangel and to the situation at The Refuge. He also had something important to add to the information the knight was seeking from them.

"Sir Trevelan, I was, in my former life, a very unsavory character, you might say. And you would be correct. I was one of two men who held down Master Greatworth while he was bein tortured. His death was a foregone affair. Somehow, the grace of God fell on my whole company of Rovers and we were forever transformed from the awful life we formerly led. It was Evangel and the hermit here who became the instruments and means of strippin the lies away from us. It was as the bard told us tonight.

"My companions and I have become part of hers and Matthew's family," Óengus tried explaining more, but he fell short of words.

"I understand Master Scanlan, what you are saying, perhaps more than you know or realize," said the knight gently. "Did you or Brother Matthew place someone in charge of The Refuge before you came here to the Priory?"

"Aye, Matthew did so. He appointed our lead tracker, William Valarin, that position."

246

"Can you rely on him?" asked Sir Trevelan.

"Yes," Scanlan and the hermit said together.

The knight smiled at them both. "I understand the conflict in which my plan places you. When we are through with our business here, I will send a company of some of my best builders and engineers. We will help build a better road into The Refuge and provide assistance in your rebuilding plans. How does that sound to you?"

Evangel replied, "It sounds too good to be true, Sir Knight. What purpose does all of your aid to Matthew, Óengus and me fulfill?"

The knight smiled, and then laughed good–naturedly. "Why, Lady, I do believe in the brief time I have known you that you can include me as one of your many converts and believers to your faith in the Lord and to the Risen One, as you call him."

Evangel looked at the knight closely to determine the sincerity of his words. "Sir Trevelan, I pray that you are not being in jest with me as I think part of your nature compels you to be."

"Nay, Lady, I am neither playing a buffoon to you nor treating you as one. The truth of my statement stands as a testimony to the power you represent."

"Grandfather, what do you think? What does the good Lord tell you we must do?"

The hermit looked at Evangel. He turned to the knight and stated, "So be it said."

"So be it finished," the Champion of the Realm intoned.

True to his word, Sir Trevelan's plan was scrupulously carried out in the manner he shared with Evangel. Captain Vallans and twenty of his men escorted her, Matthew, Óengus and the Finleys back to where they had stayed in the stone house the night before. Guard duty was assigned to fifteen men in four two-hour shifts. The shifts were brief and helped guarantee that the men stayed alert during their time at watch. The short length of this duty also permitted them to get more rest, especially in comparison to their being assigned an average three to four hours shift.

The Finleys retired for the evening almost as soon as they arrived at his office. As they were walking up to the second floor, Matthew followed them to the bottom of the stairs. Looking up at their retreating forms, he worriedly advised them saying, "Finley, I think you had best go along with us in the morning to the High King's court. This place is no longer safe for you and your family either."

The couple stopped almost at the top of the stairs.

248

Matthew could see them outlined in the light of the candle Mrs. Finley was holding in her hands.

"I'm inclined to agree with you, brother," he tiredly responded. "Let me sleep on it, or at least let me get some brief rest and mayhap the dawn of a new day will give Mrs. Finley and me a fresh perspective."

"That sounds wise," The hermit said. "Good night."

Finley nodded his head as if Matthew could see him do that.

Mrs. Finley vocalized his thoughts by saying, "Good night as well to you Master Matthew. God bless you for what you, Evangel and Óengus have done here in the priory for all of us."

"Thank you as well, Mrs. Finley, for hosting us here in this beautiful place."

Matthew watched them climb the rest of the way to the top of the stairs. He turned to go back to Evangel and Óengus as the older couple disappeared into the second floor corridor.

Upon his return to Finley's office space, he sat down at the table where they were already seated.

They talked about the extraordinary events of the day.

Evangel yawned and said, "I cannot go to sleep until you both tell me of your responses to the Bard Somairhle's performance."

Matthew deferred his answer to Óengus.

The young man bowed his head deep in thought. After reflecting a bit on what he was going to say, he answered, "I don't know what to say because I never was exposed to anythin like that except for the day the three wolves became wind, flames and kings and when I went to find Captain Tabard." He stopped and looked at Evangel for her reaction to what he had just said.

"I think I understand what you are saying. But, please, tell me more what you mean," she encouraged him.

"It was not normal," he sheepishly said. "I'm not sure I understood what he was doin or sayin, but it was a powerful performance, nevertheless. The music and the words put me under a spell. I'm not sure what kind of spell. I hope it was not a harmful one to you or to any of us."

"Thank you, Óengus, I think I felt the same way about it," she said. "Grandfather, what did you think about it?"

"I think we saw a very politically astute poet direct a powerful message to the clergy, nobility, and the soldiery in the Great Hall tonight. Without question, he is a grand master at his craft. I have seldom seen, or even heard of, the like of it. His performance will haunt the clergy for a long time, and it sent a galvanizing message for people to seek alternative visions and answers over our current times. Why, lass, what did you think about it?"

"It was magical, disturbing, and I did not want it to end. Somehow it felt as though he stopped time itself for but a moment. I am tired. I think I need to sleep, first; then I can better answer you tomorrow."

"Fair enough, Evangel," Matthew said. "I think we should all retire for the night. Dawn arrives very soon tomorrow morning."

Matthew found three candles and lit them. As he did the night before, he handed one to Óengus and the other to Evangel. The young man said his good night to them and walked to his bedroom. Matthew and Evangel each went to their own room on the second floor.

This time when three rooms, plus the Finley's, were lit by candlelight, those outside watching these candles shed their respective light, were there to protect rather than to subject those inside to harm.

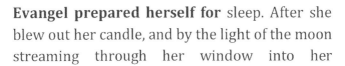

Evangel prepared herself for sleep. After she blew out her candle, and by the light of the moon streaming through her window into her bedroom, she took off her shawl and then her well-made leather shoes. She then slipped out of the beautiful dress she had been wearing. She folded it neatly and placed it on the chair in her room that was next to the bed, while the shawl was doubled over and placed on the top of the chair's cresting rail. She put her shoes together underneath the chair.

Leaving her linen undergarment on, she knelt before the bed and said her prayers. When she finished she lifted the bedcovers aside and got onto the bed. She closed her eyes. To her surprise and annoyance, she could not immediately go to sleep. She kept reviewing the day's events over and over.

She got up from the bed and walked over to the side of the window. Kneeling down, Evangel looked out at the moon and wondered if any of those remaining at The Refuge were looking at it as well. She worried about Captain Tabard's health; she hoped he was recovering from his journey to the fen, and she was concerned about who was taking care of him.

Feeling as though she might be able to go to sleep, she got back into bed and looked up at the ceiling. She thought about the Bard Diarmad Somairhle's performance and tried to puzzle it out in her mind. *I've got to share with Grandfather what I thought about it, but I don't know what it was. How do you explain to someone what you don't know, or even understand?*

She recalled how the man who ushered them to their tables in the Great Hall looked like the bard. *Was it him?* She questioned herself. *Why would he do that? I mean, Sir Trevelan said that the bard isolated himself from everyone else, stayed alone in his room and concentrated on preparing for his performance. Was the knight telling me the truth, or was he adding to the poet's mystery and allure of reputation?*

She smiled to herself and thought that what he had done was mischievous. *Being an usher and next to the announcer allowed him to get a good look at his audience and to learn how people were acting before his performance. He got to see the interaction between the Prioress' table and the one where we sat at.*

Before she realized it, she fell asleep in the middle of her meditations on the bard.

In her dream, when she first became aware of it, she found herself walking in a part of the woods next to The Refuge with which she was not familiar. The earth was damp and in places the surface of the ground was exposed. Patches of grass and bare soil conjoined with one another. It was windy and it had just rained.

She heard something in a thicket of hazel, poplar and willow that gave off a rasping, almost whimpering, noise. She listened closer to it and became convinced it was Wheezer making the sound.

"But it can't be my puppy, because he's become a whirlwind," she said aloud.

Again she heard the same sound, but it reached her awareness with a sense of greater harshness, *perhaps even urgency.* Not concerned any longer with making any sense about what was happening, she got on her hands and knees and went into the thicket to discover the source of the ambiguous dissonance.

She laughed out loud as she was trying to crawl into and through the thicket. "If whatever is calling for help is whimpering, then it can't be Wheezer, as it must be Whimper!"

Going further in and almost to the center, she thought she saw something white. She hurried to reach it. When she arrived at the place where she saw something move, she realized with a shock that she had come upon three common vipers intertwining with one another. They were all thick–bodied and had black and startling white diamond, zigzag markings all around their backs and undersides. Their heads were large and their expressions shone with a grim looking intelligence. They had rounded snouts that they were delightfully using to rub one another as they were laughing about, and talking to one another regarding, the bard's performance.

Seeing her tumble into their area, they stopped moving and reared up at her as one. The one in the middle said to her in a slightly tinged, sibilant voice, "What is it with you, human child, that you so rudely must interrupt our sport with one another?"

Taken aback from what she was seeing, she did not speak to them.

"Ah," exclaimed the one to her left, "She acts stung with our venom without yet being consumed by our bite!"

The one on her right added, "No cat has her tongue, but perhaps the bard stole it, instead."

More laughter greeted her as the three before her started twisting around one another.

For some reason, their laughter sparked a fury in her that she did not stop to consider. "As snakes, you seem awfully content with yourselves," she hissed at them.

Surprised at her response, they leaned over toward her in the denseness and closeness of the thicket.

She involuntarily closed her eyes and braced herself for their bite, but none came.

She quickly opened her eyes and saw that she was just below the Bard's stone dais in the priory's Great Hall. In the place where the snakes were just an instant before rested the poet's harp, the same spot where he had played it earlier in the evening. Feeling more danger emanate from the harp than she did the three vipers, she sprang back from it.

The harp, first laughing as the snakes, changed its register by a series of sliding notes that sounded like chants, cloth being ripped, mice squeaking behind a wall, and the scream of a deer being brought down by wolves.

The sounds stopped and were replaced by a steel ringing voice that questioned her, "Mortal child, so you presume to enter my home: As you are here, what dost thou intend to do in my presence?"

"I am trying to sleep, Lady, not bother you with my presence," she answered.

"Humpf," the harp snorted in a bass chording combination. As it talked to her, its strings vibrated with no player's hands placing them into motion. "I have destroyed others lesser and greater than you out of mere spite. I speak not from an abuse of my power, but out of the fact that you are trespassing in a place where you do not belong."

It chortled again in a glissando of notes that felt as if it were tearing a piece of her heart out. She wanted to fall to the ground and whimper like the sound she heard upon waking into this dream.

Three of the strings that were fastened to the string rib in the center of the harp slipped themselves away from their grommets and started to whip out at her.

Just before they snapped into her face, a strong, masculine looking hand reached out and grabbed them firmly. "Not now, my children," a familiar sounding voice intoned, "You need to mind your temper and your manners. This child is our guest and the rules of hospitality must apply or we forfeit our right to be here."

The harp shook itself and grumbled, but the strings reattached themselves to their original places in the middle of its sisters and brothers' strings.

Evangel looked closely at the speaker and realized it was the usher who had just saved her from being marked by the sting of the strings.

He bowed grandly to her and with a smile said, "You must excuse the agitation of the harp. She is very territorial and, frankly, quite imperious. As she is her own sentient being, she has a sense of ownership that is magisterial: it

257

extends into the material world as it does into the ethereal." The harp played off key chords and struck a discordant phrase in counterpoint to the usher's last comment.

The notes hit the floor and sparked away near where she stood looking up at it.

"You must forgive me, Lady Evangel. The announcer is not here and I have been amiss in not introducing you to her. Her name in her native tongue is Cébhfhionn. I would use that name in formal situations or times. Informally, I affectionately call her my "Fair Haired One". Thus, Lady Evangel Blessingvale, it is with great pride that I introduce to you the serene muse of my inspiration, Cébhfhionn."

Evangel bowed to the harp's genius saying, "It is an honor to be introduced to you. Pray forgive any blunder in my manners or the failings of human indiscretion that I have given you."

Cébhfhionn purred out a thank you to the poet for the introduction and in meeting Evangel formally. Unknown to the young woman, Cébhfhionn ranged through three different modes of musical systems, moving from a Lydian tonal scale, to a Phrygian one; and, closing her statement in a Dorian acknowledgement.

The usher laughed in appreciation of what the harp performed for them. Looking at the harp, then at Evangel, he said, "She is quite pleased with herself."

"How do you know that *she* is?" the young woman asked.

"She's putting on a show of her talent, shall we say. I think she likes you."

Even though Cébhfhionn had been singing in a language to Evangel that she did not comprehend, the young woman nevertheless felt she understood that *The Fair Haired One* had forgiven her and that there was a sense from the harp that she was glad to meet Evangel.

Cébhfhionn poured out several more phrases of dulcet tones, the pitch of the notes blending with one another in a refreshing shower of musical rain.

The usher ran his hand through his hair, smiled and gave a genuine laugh, "I agree with you, my love, the young human child understands your intent. I am glad that you like her now."

He gave Evangel his right elbow for her to take it in hand.

She took it and he walked with her away from the stone dais. He led her back through the thicket with far greater ease and comfort than when she first entered it.

Strange, she thought to herself, *I do not have to crawl out as I had to do to get in here.*

Getting to the end of the thicket, they next began walking through a corridor that was both in the forest and was enshrouded in fog at the same time. Being in this space gave her the feeling she was at a great height in the sky. They walked by a variety of scenes from her past, as well as images from her present, that were placed in various levels on the "walls". She felt like she was looking at familiar figures, features and forms that were woven into remarkably lifelike looking tapestries.

At last, the hall passage disappeared and she was in an area below a hill that loomed ahead of her. There was sound of profound grieving coming from the top of the hill. It was a deeper and eerier form of lament than she first heard, and she mistakenly first thought it was caused, again, by one of her wolves being in distress. She walked up the hill and deeper into the sound of mourning.

Interspersed with this suffering of pain and sorrow, she heard men laughing and gambling with dice. She could hear the individual die being collectively shaken against one another in a metal cup of some sort. The sound of it seemed a contradiction: part of it was hollow, greasy and foul to her, while the other was sharp, concise and greedily vied for her attention. The closer she approached the top of the hill the more she slowed her own steps. She knew now what she was going towards and she did not want to experience such anguish.

Arriving irrevocably at the top of the hill, she saw three crosses. She inherently knew that a great amount of blood had been shed, and that severe physical pain and punishment had been inflicted specifically on one of the three who hung there. When she was able to take a look at the one with a sign on the tree upon which he was tied and impaled, everything around him, including the soldiers gambling below on the ground, people in various groups looking at the horrid scene, the soldier picking up a spear of destiny with which to run him through, all froze and came to a stop. There was utter and relentless silence.

She came closer to the one with the sign above him. She stopped before his place of torment. The wind sighed around the delimbed tree from which he hung. The clouds hung low as well and dripped their own agony onto the ground. She saw that his head was down onto his chest. He was not moving at all.

He has died and is no more. But I know this cannot be. Why is he so still?

She felt the usher near her. In the corner of her eyes she noticed he was wearing a white robe. She turned to look at him. The usher had gone. In his place, stood the Bard of the Realm of the Western Isles.

"Why is the Lord frozen in place? Is he dead?"

"Nay, Lady, He is between time and eternity at the moment. He is doing what His Father asks of Him."

"Standing here in front of Him is too much for me; I cannot take it. I will die doing so."

"Indeed, Lady Evangel, as we all will and must."

"Is there any hope left in the world, poet?"

"Always, my Lady, no matter the darkness around us, and in us, too."

"Will he arise from this wood?"

"Nay, His suffering must reach its earthly closure in the finality of the body, soul and spirit being crushed by sin."

Unbidden, tears started falling from her eyes.

The bard looked at her with compassion. Tears also fell from his.

"Why must goodness always perish?" she managed to ask.

"While it does appear to cease in its living form, it inflicts a heavy toll not only on those who remain behind, but on the forces arrayed against its very presence."

"You are avoiding answering my question, Bard Somairhle: *Why must the best amongst us go down into defeat?*"

"I cannot give you a satisfactory answer, Lady, because in life we summon too much denial into our awareness. It's not just goodness and beauty that are defeated, but the nature of our world also is ground into the clay of reality. Everything in this time becomes defeated. Everything in this life is crushed. Nothing in it is immortal except for those who put their trust in His death."

"Are you saying that an exchange of some kind is being made between the powers at play?"

"Yes, a most terrible price is being paid. It is beyond our capacity to withstand it and understand it. There is so much purity, strength and honor in Him that it serves as a passage to another life, another world, another connection away from the hunger eroding our hearts' deep joy."

Evangel had reached a breaking point where she felt another moment in this place would slay her. She was about to protest when she realized she was no longer on the hill of the slain.

Instead, she found herself on a battlefield looking at a young man in the prime of his life fighting to stay alive.

CHAPTER TWENTY-ONE

He carried a two–edged, falchion sword. It shone as though it radiated its own light. It was like a star falling in the middle of the night. Instead of disappearing out of sight, this light was moving in rapid parries, strikes, counterstrikes, overhand and underhand movements at blinding speeds. The sword moved as if under its own volition. It reminded her of the bard and his harp: both needed to be as one to render and summon together their combined mastery of the spoken word, song and melody.

The man and the sword being used in combat before her seemed to operate, *Nay, dance in dread performance before me*, in a similar fashion. One was not as effective without the other. They seemed to teach one another what was needed at the moment. However, as she observed them further, the sword intimated to the warrior the strategy he could use not only against his immediate opponent, but those soon to be in hand–to–hand contact with him.

The sword flared, sparked off the weapons brought against it. It snapped metal apart and flayed open armor as though it were cheese being sliced for a rabid company of uninvited and demon–starved diners. Without question, there was no polite company here. Men were locked into the embrace and dance of war. The man and his sword, like the bard and his harp, evinced a purity of performance, a rendition of mastery that was befuddling to witness. While one poured out the grief and joy of life, the other drenched those opposed to him in death. The warrior and his fighting prowess puzzled and fascinated friend and foe alike. He swept all those before him away in a fatal, effortless melody of its wielder's discretion and of the sword's own conquering effulgence.

The hand and arm wielding it were not overtly muscular. The warrior himself was an average looking man. Brown eyes, auburn hair, short red beard and square features. He was in superb physical condition. Again, watching him fight, she could not tell what was the more formidable weapon, the sword, or the man himself. She decided that it was a verity the one needed the other and, thus, they worked as a team together.

His allies and his enemies fighting around him sought to be near him, to share in the fervor of his battle ardor and to be within the glare and gaze of his eyes. Men screamed, cheered, grunted, bled, were torn asunder, disappeared in the sweep of annihilation occurring around him.

A lull occurred in the area of combat where he and his companions had been fighting. He seemed to have vast reserves of energy and fortitude. The men fighting at his side with him leaned on their swords, pikes, and spears, too exhausted to speak at first. A rallying cry began, despite their battle enervation. They congratulated one another. They exulted in the fact that they were whole, still alive, and filled with complete fervor and zeal to make their mark on this field of combat in such a unique and fell way.

Evangel was able to observe what the young man was wearing in some detail. She could see that what he had on was made with great skill and care. His armor was made of cured and hardened leather. She could see it because of the many slices that had bitten deeply into the leather from the weapons arrayed against him by the young man's foes. The leather was wrapped over by very thin plates of hardened steel and stitched together with great mastery to create a highly effective, yet lightweight, suit of armor.

One of his companions approached him. "Well, Sergeant Warren, we beat them down to nothing. But their commanders don't care; there's plenty more of them they can send against us. And I'm concerned that the next wave of attack is one that will comprise numbers we will not be able to handle."

The young man named Warren smiled easily.

Evangel's heart skipped a beat seeing him smile. His laugh, light and free, conquered her heart.

"Well, de Ashton," the young man responded, "being the onions that we are, we'll peel back as many layers as we can from them. Tears *will* be spilled: Our swords will cry for their deaths. Their deaths will cry out from our swords. It will become very expensive for their commanders to take this field."

Warren's other companions flocked around him, consternation written on their faces.

"We're not going to get out of this one, Pall, no matter what prayer or strategy you use," said a man to Pall's left.

"The numbers are against us, Sergeant," said a third companion. "We're just a vanguard the High Marshall sent out to check out the rumors of raiders massing against us in this section of the realm."

"Aye," Warren said to them almost nonchalantly, "when they hit us again, we go into battle squares. We'll grind them against the squares for as long as we can."

Evangel became startled when Somairhle touched his hand on her elbow. The vision of the young man on his field of combat started to fade even though she thought she was right there in the field with him.

"Evangel," a voice only she heard said.

She could not hear what the young sergeant was saying to his men. She shook her head as if the motion in making the physical movement would help restore her ability to hear his voice, and clear the one away from calling her.

"Evangel," the same voice spoke her name again.

The young woman again chose to ignore the voice calling within her mind. She became hopeful that the scene was not passing her by because she was still able to hear horns being blown. She turned to see where the war horns were located. She quickly discovered that their woeful cries marked out the enemy's position.

For they are the enemy, she thought to herself convincingly, *they oppose this young man and his command.*

Men were massing at the opposite end of the field. Ranks of infantry were in the middle of their formation, with cavalry flanking them on either end. Each of the units was commanded by their captains who stood at the front of the battle line.

"Evangel," the voice spoke her name for the third time.

"Yes?" she asked aloud. "Who is speaking to me?"

The opposing force of warriors began to charge the few hundred or so companions surrounding Pall Warren. Cavalry on both sides veered away from the charging ranks of infantry. She saw that they planned to attack Pall on his left and right sides, perhaps even encircle him completely.

"He needs your help," the voice responded.

Implicitly knowing who the voice was referring to, she simply said, "Tell me what I must do."

"You already know, Child of the World," was its answer.

Pall, with the aid of de Ashton, helped oversee his men get into formation. Instead of using a defensive one, as the enemy would expect him to use, he employed an offensive one. He placed the men in two phalanxes, with each one containing fifty men. With their shields joined to one another, their long spears extended over their shields, while still providing cover for the men in front. She watched the files close and grew worried that there were not enough of them to make the phalanxes deeper.

269

The charge of the enemy rapidly attacking them had covered half the length of the field.

The sergeant saw that there were enough men still left to make up two squadrons. Warren and de Ashton helped expedite the process of their forming up and moving into their places on the far left and right sides of the heavily armed men in the middle of them.

"Evangel," the voice urged her.

In her mind's eye, she saw what was going to happen to these few men waiting for the final charge to overwhelm them. Of the men remaining with Pall, no one was going to be left alive. Feeling selfish for desiring only to save one man, she hesitated in interceding on his behalf only. However, the pressure and the insistence of the voice calling her helped give her the impetus to help Sergeant Warren.

"Concentrate on placing the three strings in the center of the harp in motion," the inner voice advised aloud.

She knew now that the Harp Cébhfhionn, was the Risen One's Lyre. In one fluid motion she threw her hands and arms out toward Pall's direction.

Contact between the two armed opponents was imminent and about to occur.

She prayed for his protection. She said, "Please, Lord, take not his life. Take away his awareness of who he is, if you must."

Evangel felt her shoulders shudder.

Pall's men counterattacked the onrushing enemy and made brutal contact with them.

She paused in her petition for Pall's safety, as the ground underneath her feet trembled. Rising up and continuing through her feet, legs, body and flowing up into her arms, was a single wave of energy. She felt it course through her forearms, wrists and hands.

The two massed phalanxes punched through the oncoming charge and went deeply into its center. The grim work of killing, begun in earnest, increased in its furor.

Words formed in her spirit at the same time the wave of energy exploded from the palms and fingertips of her hands, "I beg of you, forgive me of my failings. Save him; let him fight for you. May you appoint him one of your champions."

An oscillating wave of energy burst toward Pall. Out of the corner of his eyes, he saw it rapidly approaching him. It looked like three arrows of wind spinning around its center. As this revolving undulation passed over the tops of the trees, it flung their crowns into wild gyration. Three distinct sounds registered on the human ear. Of the humans present, only Pall, Evangel and the poet heard them.

He glanced up quickly again at the source of what he thought was another attack. Looking in her direction, he saw her standing in the air above him. He turned fully now and faced her, ignoring the slaughter going on around him.

Their eyes made contact with one another.

Something deeply within the frame of their being shook itself, arose into their perception and sealed an understanding between them that rendered itself as an eternal promise of loyalty.

Pall stumbled, stood up and became inundated, engulfed into the craw and gullet of combat.

Before the vision she was seeing completely passed from her view, she heard him say only one word of a command he was giving his men:

"Aeonians..."

———————

She awoke to darkness and predawn bird song. For a moment, she was not quite sure of her location. The reality of the dream still gripped her sense of awareness too firmly. Little by little, and with some regret, she moved from dream to wakefulness. She waited to arise from her bed until the dawn light lit her room faintly. Getting up from her bed when the darkness dissipated into the all but faint forms of reality around her, she dressed in the clothes she first wore in arriving at the priory. She heard her grandfather passing by her door and his greeting of good morning to the Finleys.

She went to open the door and as her hand lifted its latch, something light fell from it onto her left wrist and then to the floor. Evangel felt as though something had stung or bit her. Curious, even anxious, to know what had touched her, she went over to the nightstand next to the bed to retrieve her candle. Lighting it with a slight tremor in her hands, she brought it over to the door to see what she could find as evidence that something tangible, indeed, had startled her.

As soon as the light from the candle was cast on the floorboards near the door, she spied the culprit that had come in contact with her. She leaned over and picked it up. When she realized what she was holding in her hand, she almost dropped it again. In her hand were three harp strings in the form of a bracelet, twisted and knotted around one another like a single plait of hair. *Or*, she thought, *three common vipers*.

Out loud, Evangel muttered, "Maybe they will rear up and start laughing at me."

She opened her bedroom door, stepped out into the hallway and followed the reassuring echo of the Finleys' voices going down the wooden stairs into the office.

273

When she arrived in Finley's office, Matthew, Óengus, the Finleys and Sir Trevelan were in the room talking quietly with one another.

"Good morn, lass," Matthew greeted her. "What is it that you have in your hand?"

"I think it is from part of the dream I had last night," she answered. She placed the plait of intertwined strings in front of her grandfather onto the table at which he was sitting.

When Matthew fully realized what she had placed before him, he drew a deep breath and said, "Lord's Mercy, these are three of the center strings from the Priméces' harp!"

Upon hearing the substance of the hermit's comment, everyone gathered around him. Each one present in the room, except for Evangel and Matthew asked to hold the harp strings in his or her hands.

Evangel, upon their urging and questioning her about the strings, told them her dream several times over. When she was done sharing with them what she could recall from the dream, she turned to Matthew and said, "Before I retired for the night, Grandfather, you asked me what I thought of the bard's performance. At that time I could not answer your question because I did not know what I thought of it. I was overwhelmed by his performance, and I believed I was too tired to respond properly to your wanting to know my opinion about the virtue of what he achieved in the Great Hall."

She looked over at Sir Trevelan who was now holding the harp strings in his right hand.

"Perhaps," she continued to explain, "those three strings you hold in your hand, Sir Knight, provide the best answer that I can give to you, Grandfather."

"Lady, I believe that you have been given many priceless gifts throughout your young life, and especially in recent days. The one I hold in my hand that has been bequeathed to you by the Muse of the Harp, Cébhfhionn, and inspired by the artistry, vigilance and guidance of the High King's Ri–Eigeas, point all the more to my accompanying you and yours to the Royal Court."

Óengus, who had been in great wonder and amazement over the harp's strings being wrapped onto her bedroom door's latch said, "Evangel, at least twice now you have seen and been in the presence of the Risen One. I am not a cleric, and I am not an educated man, but I believe you, and all of us who are near you and care for you, need to better understand what it is we must needs be doing. I think that Sir Trevelan's suggestion to accompany and introduce us to the High King and his court has strong and powerful merit to it."

The knight cleared his throat and made a promise to them, "Not only will that occur dear Lady, if I may address you in such a manner, but I swear a vow to you and yours that you have my protection and ward for as long as I breathe, and for as long as I have the strength and capacity to ensure your safety and wellbeing."

Evangel looked at the High King's Champion and bowed to him as the bard had done the night before when just the knight and the bard were the only ones remaining standing in the hall before the performance began.

Seeing her gesture, Sir Trevelan laughed and said, "I think you will do well in the High King's Court."

For a moment, the stress and rush of events were forgotten. People joined the knight in laughter. When their fast had been broken and they had eaten the food before them, Sir Trevelan gathered them together to tell them his plan for the day.

"Earlier than I promised before, Brother Matthew, a company of my men, experts in building, road construction and farming will be sent to The Refuge. Rather than sending them there later on sometime after we reach the High King's Court, it is better to deploy them while we are nearby your hermitage. I will have them assess what needs to be done and send them all the necessary equipment, tools and manpower needed to achieve their counsel and advice once they send me word of their needs.

"The rest of the people in my contingent who are not soldiers have gone on ahead to where my battalion is encamped. Two companies of men remain with me outside the front door to Finley's quarters.

"Finley, you need to gather your family together, bring only essential items with you and depart from the Priory with us. The Prioress will not allow you to live here, let alone stay alive, after I and my men leave this place.

"I will be going to the room below the Buttery and bring out the sisters Muriel and Juliana. They also will accompany you to the High Court. We will not be denied or stopped. There are too many of us and our arms are far superior against those of the clerical guard. Does all of what I have just shared with you meet with your consent?"

Matthew spoke for them all, "Sir Trevelan, your actions are representative of everything knighthood stands for and represents. It is an honor and a blessing that you have given me and mine, the Finleys, and even this priory, by your presence and your charity to strangers such as us. I think it is time we cease our planning and put them now into action."

16

The knight nodded to the hermit.

Finley asked, "What of those who do not wish to stay here and desire to leave with us as well. Can we help them do so?"

Sir Trevelan smiled, "I thought of that very same question after you left the priory last night to return here for the remainder of the evening. Half the battalion will be arriving at St. Åyrwyus, hopefully, around noon to midafternoon. Those who wish to go with us as you have pointed out to me, Master Finley, are welcome to do so. What vehicles, horses, mules, tack, supplies and other fundamental equipment and food that are here, and can be used to help these folk leave with us, will be wise to employ. Combined with our own resources, we should be able to move everyone that wishes to do so with us at the end of the day. I would like at least three to four hours of daylight left for us to travel away from the priory today."

A knock resounded on the front door.

Óengus went over to it and opened it wide. Seeing it was Captain Vallans, he waved him on inside.

The Captain walked over to his commander, saluted and informed him, "Everything is all set and ready to put in motion, Sir Trevelan."

"Excellent, Captain Vallans. We are preparing to leave almost momentarily. However, as I mentioned to you earlier this morning when I arrived, we will not be leaving right away after we free the two sisters. Mr. Finley, here, is putting out an invitational call to all those in the priory who wish to return to the High Court with us. There are still many estates, and even empty manors and priories themselves in the Realm, which can comfortably house those who want to leave here. Pray see to the men outside as well as to those eventually arriving. I will be going to free the two sisters from here."

Mrs. Finley left to go get her children and any other family members who wished to leave with her and her husband. Finley also left to gather his men together to invite people to move away from the priory grounds.

Matthew, Evangel and Óengus left the stone house with Sir Trevelan.

A pair of roan horses hitched to a sturdy wagon behind them was waiting for Evangel.

The same steeds Matthew and Óengus rode yesterday were patiently waiting for their expected riders next to the wagon.

When everyone was ready to depart from the stone house, the knights on their destriers, their respective squires and the column of men gathered there with them and their attendants, all marched forward toward the priory in a solemn cavalcade.

Sir Trevelan rode over to where Evangel was riding on the wagon. "Here, my Lady," he said, "I think this is yours," and he proffered her the three strings from the bard's harp.

"Thank you, Sir Trevelan," she said.

"I return it to you with the condition that you show this extraordinary gift to the High King, and that you tell him the story of it," the knight suggested to her.

"Gladly!" she exclaimed. "Will the poet be there with us?" she asked.

The knight laughed and said, "Verily: and I believe he will help announce and usher you before High King Peter Áed Menn Rochtmar."

The knight ceased from his levity and said to her, "In all sincerity, Lady Evangel, you are not the only one who was inspired and blessed by the Risen One last night. While you saw this mighty warrior you bespoke of so highly, I was told in a vision He gave me to seek out his father."

Hearing his statement, Evangel found that she could hardly breathe. She felt she was back in the middle of the battlefield when she first saw Pall smile and laugh with the grace and ease of pure freedom and strength.

Not trusting her voice, she hesitated, then said, "Yes, Sir Trevelan, please continue. Why do you wish to inquire after the warrior's father?"

"Because, my Lady, he was a famous warrior, in turn, and high commander in his own right. He lives in the realm directly to our east."

She looked doubtfully at this news, "How is seeing this man pertinent to me, kind Sir?"

"He no longer fights on the field of combat, or commands thousands of troops."

"What does he do now, instead?" she inquired.

"He is one of the finest blacksmiths ever known in this part of the world."

"Aye, Sir Trevelan, and what of this man?"

"Lady Evangel, I believe that you are the jewel that is in the heart of this Realm. God's Spirit is bringing you onto His path in this regard. You are a warrior for the Risen One. The Lord told me that this Master Smith, whose name is David Warren, is to make a suit of armor and a sword for you such as he made for his son Pall."

Evangel felt a shock of recognition overwhelm her. Of all the words that the knight had used in talking to her, she only really heard Pall's name mentioned. She gave no outward sign of this perception to anyone around her. She looked at the knight next to her and the long column of men on foot and those on their horses marching down the road to an unknown, yet very palpable and ostensible future.

She became lost in thought. Her right hand fingers, independent of her conscious mind, entwined the three harp strings around the wrist of her left hand.

Upon seeing Evangel wrap Cébhfhionn's heart strings around her wrist, the High King's Champion of the Realm smiled.

End of *THE PENITENT – PART II*

CAST OF CHARACTERS

Ailwin Athdar: The Abbot of **Dawn's Abbey**, a monastery for men located in the Vale of Naomhin in the Western Isles.

Abigail, Edward and Adam: Three of the seven children of Finley and Mrs. Finley.

Cébhfhionn (also known as "**Fair Locks**"): The name of **Bard Diarmad Somairhle's** harp. This harp is considered one of the chief instruments of the **Risen One**.

Sir Trevelan du Coeur: The High King's Champion of the Realm. He becomes the protector and sponsor of **Evangel Blessingvale** and her adopted grandfather, the hermit **Matthew Greatworth**.

Constance and her daughter **Francis:** Constance is in charge of the sisters' laundry at **St. Åyrwyus Priory**. The night of the performance by Bard Diarmad Somairhle, she and her daughter brought a soft blue dress, a matching shawl and a pair of leather shoes to Evangel. Constance is a close friend of **Mrs. Finley**.

Edward: A serf who labors for St. Åyrwyus Priory.

Finley & Mrs. Finley: Finley is the Master Groundskeeper for St. Åyrwyus Priory. He and his wife have seven children of which three are named in the story, these being Adam, Abigail and Edward. Although Finley is no longer a cleric, he and Matthew Greatworth took their brotherly vows together.

Henry Fulk: A member of the guard at St. Åyrwyus Priory.

Gisela, Nesta & Emma: Mrs. Finley's peers; where they live and work on the grounds of St. Åyrwyus Priory. All three women are mothers as well.

Evangel Greatworth (also known as "**the Lady from the Wood**" or "**the Lady of the Fields and Forest**"): Her adopted grandfather, Matthew Greatworth, gave her this name: after finding her placed in a ditch for safety by her mother from outlaws. Both her parents and the members of their caravan were brutally murdered.

Her first name means "Good News". Throughout the Western Isles, her birth name has been combined interchangeably with her given and last names.

Evangel Blessingvale, under the sponsorship of Sir Trevelan du Coeur and the auspices of the **High King and Queen** of the realm, united the military forces to defend its sovereignty, which is under domestic and foreign attack. Her charismatic qualities, spiritual depth and direct connection with the Risen One have made her a driving force of reform in the Western Isles.

Matthew Greatworth: A deeply religious hermit who lives in **The Refuge**, a cabin in the deep woods, which he built by himself almost half a century ago. He calls the surrounding forest, **God's Temple**. He is a holy man who secretly has worshipped the Risen One for most of his life.

Colin Hays: The youngest member of the former **Dread Rovers**; he held a noose over Matthew Greatworth's neck when he and his fellow outlaws first trespassed on The Refuge and tortured the hermit.

Julia: She is an oblate sister at St. Åyrwyus Priory, and one of Evangel's closest friends.

Terric Lovell: The Rover who was killed and brought back to life by Evangel.

Marta Matasan: The Prioress of St. Åyrwyus Priory. She is in league with malefactors and revolutionaries, domestic and foreign, seeking to destroy the political, spiritual and social orders of the realm.

Muriel: She is a Sister of St. Åyrwyus Priory. She is Evangel's longtime friend, confidante and advisor.

High King Peter Áed Menn Rochtmar: The High King of the Western Isles.

High Queen Isolde Bébhinn Menn Rochtmar: The High Queen of the Western Isles.

The Risen One: A reference to the spiritual reality known on **old Earth** as **the Messiah**, **Yeshuah Hamashiach**, or **Jesus the Christ**. His name, personage and divinity have been banned by the major religious orders in the Western Isles, West Fündländ and other contemporary realms. Severe, to capital, punishment is meted out to those who mention His name and/or worship Him and follow His teachings.

Sauria: An off–world being and leader of the **Slayers**.

Óengus Scanlan: A Rover who single–handedly helped rescue the tracking party sent out to find and bring **Captain Osbert Tabard** back to The Refuge. He is one of three men who had held down Matthew when the Dread Rovers first entered The Refuge and tortured Greatworth. Scanlan becomes one of the hermit's closest allies.

Sean: The overseer for the fruit trees and berry shrubs at St. Åyrwyus Priory. Excluding **Finley**, he was the first of the laborers to speak with Óengus Scanlan at the priory when Evangel, Matthew and Scanlan visited there.

Slayers: Off–world beings, their connection to human beings is a mysterious and deeply disturbing one. Most humans look upon them as evil, or at best as tricksters and troublemakers. They have been known to haunt areas where they visit or take up residence for varying amounts of time. People have been tortured, kidnapped and gone missing when contact is made with them. Few return. All survivors are deeply and seemingly irreparably changed, exhibiting profound and psychotic personality and behavioral changes.

Diarmad Somairhle: One of the Western Isles greatest bards in its history. He was given the formal title of "**the Ri–Eigeas, the Priméces, the Bard of the Realm of the Western Isles, Filidhe Diarmad Somairhle**". His mastery of his craft is legendary.

The musical, psychological and spiritual connection he has with his harp, **Cébhfhionn**, is recondite, mystical and transcends normal human abilities and understandings. Although relatively unknown, bard and harp have a longstanding relationship with the Risen One.

Captain Osbert Tabard: Captain of the **Dread Rovers**, he experiences and endures life changing transformations from being an outlaw, experiencing a spiritual conversion and undergoing contact with Sauria and his slayers at the fen near The Refuge. Tabard becomes prescient and is given the gift of prophecy and the prophetic word.

Professor Melvin Tobin, Ph.D. (2065–2189): A former internationally known and respected professor. Upon retiring, he was unanimously granted the status of emeritus professor by his peers at Harvard University in Cambridge, Massachusetts on Old Earth. During his research and teaching years at Harvard, Professor Tobin held three endowed chairs in Philosophical Systems, Intelligence Engineering and Quantum Genetics. He was a specialist in evolutionary intervention.

Captain Conrad Vallans: The captain of **Sir Trevelan du Coeur's** men-at-arms.

William Valarin: The lead tracker who helped find Tabard in the fen; he was put in charge of The Refuge when Matthew, Evangel and Scanlan visited St. Åyrwyus Priory.

Pall Warren: Raised in a small village in West Fündländ by **David** and **Lucia Warren**, Pall becomes one of the finest young warriors of his time. He is especially gifted in hand–to–hand combat with the quarterstaff, falchion sword and fighting knives. He has been deeply touched by the Hand of God.

Wheezer | Whimper | Whisper: Three Flames | Three Kings of the **Risen One** appointed to serve **the Paraclete**, **the Comforter**, or **the Holy Spirit**. When first unknowingly introduced by the Risen One to Evangel and Matthew Greatworth, they are in the forms of three small, white–wolf puppies. They become transformed and revealed when Matthew is tortured, blinded and almost killed by Captain Osbert Tabard. They return in various mystical forms, one being in the guise of three, silver–grey great wolves.

Wyn: Sir Trevelan du Coeur's companion and combat horse. Wyn has carried the knight into battle many times, often saving Sir Trevelan's life.

Post a Review:

If you liked reading *THE PENITENT – PART II,* please post a review at:

immortalitywars@gmail.com

EXCERPT FROM
THE PENITENT – PART III

CHAPTER ONE

He tried not to remember what had just happened. He just did not want to see the images of ruin around him. The young man had learned, so it felt to him, that the matters of the day always intruded their tyranny over him. There was just no permanent escape from suffering. *It is always around*, he thought.

He let the walls of isolation down from around him. Myra was weeping uncontrollably. He smelled the all–pervading rot of Ünger's corpse filling his senses. A crimson, purple light radiated from the Sentinel Tree. Tom was on his knees holding Myra tightly in his arms. He had a stunned, haunted look on his face. Tears fell from his pained looking eyes. The place where Alicia was standing with Mary in her arms was literally seared away from the ground around it.

The young man became upset, then angry over the shock, evil and injustice over what just happened. He worked himself up into a furor.

Pall stood up on his feet. He walked over to where the largest piece left of the monster was still standing. Pieces of the creature were still falling away from it. On the ground was a medium–sized branch. He looked at his boots with the thought of kicking the dead body over onto the ground. Pall decided he was not as disgusted with the situation as he could have been. A more rationally held anger was returning to him. Nevertheless, he was still filled with an intense, overwhelming fury against the monster and what it had just done to mother and daughter. He picked up the bough and rammed it into the center of violence that had been Ünger.

He pushed the body just inside of the drip line, right underneath the outermost leaves of the tree. Pall then went over to the wagon. He picked up a shovel and a pitchfork. With these two tools, he gathered together as much of the rest of the demon's body that he could find.

While occupied in this task, he heard a sound that his father's forge might make when it was heating up to the desired temperature for working iron and steel. He looked over at where he had deposited the main trunk of the beast's body. Light from the crown and roots of the tree converged on it. What was left of the Ünger vibrated, became insubstantial and then just disappeared from view. The branch that had been thrust into its carcass thumped unharmed to the ground.

Occupied solely in this task of cleaning up, and observing, the foulness around him, he became vaguely aware of a tugging on his shirttail. He looked down to where something or someone was yanking at his clothing. Myra was on his left side, away from where he was holding a pitchfork full of Ünger.

"Can I help you, Pilgrim?" she asked.

He looked at her forlorn shape and turned to look at her father. Tom was on his feet, trying to take in the catastrophe around him.

Tears fell finally from Pall's eyes.

"Yes," he answered her directly and simply.

He got down on his knees and looked at her. She ran into his arms and tried to console him over her mother and sister's loss.

"Myra," he said, "you are a very brave girl. I am going to bring pieces of this thing the tree killed over to where the big one just disappeared."

"I know. I saw the tree make it go away," she said.

He nodded his head to her. "Good, don't touch them, but make sure the pieces I place around the tree are in that same spot but in a circle around the Sentinel."

"I understand, Pall," the little girl said solemnly.

Pall bent to his task. Myra watched him with complete absorption in what he was doing.

Pall heard Tom walk to the wagon and retrieve some tools. He looked over and as the light from the tree illuminated everything around it in sharp relief, he could see that Tom had picked up a shovel, saw and sledge hammer. He was carrying them out into the field, along with the branch Pall used to move the monster, where the copper beech tree could be seen in its entirety.

Pall went back to his work in cleaning up the remaining pieces of Ünger. Finishing their dual duties, Pall went to Myra and walked her over to where her father was completing what he was doing in the field.

Tom watched them approach him. When they were almost at his side he explained, "Nothin's left me and Myra from them," he pointed to the two shallow graves he had just dug. "So the least I can do is honor their memory here near this sacred tree that saved you, Myra and me from that wretched wreck of horror."

He crossed the tool head ends of the sledge hammer and shovel together to make a rough cradle for the bough he had brought over with him. He cut the branch in two and sharpened their ends into a point with the axe. Taking the two pieces of wood one at a time, the cooper used the sledge hammer to pound the sharp ends into the ground at the head of each grave. When they were set the way he wanted them, Tom reached into his pants pocket and removed a large, and a small, piece of leather from it. The cooper knelt down before the mock graves and hung the large one over the pole on his left. He said, "She would put this one in her hair and the smaller one in Mary's. It's the only thing I can think of to do...."

Tears welled up in his eyes and spilled freely down his face.

He did the same with the smaller piece of leather to his right.

Tom stood up.

Both men started to walk away back to the tree.

Myra exclaimed, "Wait, we need to say a prayer!"

Tom hung his head lower than what it was, then quickly stood up straighter. "You're right little one. I'm sorry."

"It's okay, Da," she said to him consolingly.

"Pall," Tom said, "will you say something?"

Pall took a deep breath and sighed, "Yes, gladly: it will be an honor for me to do."

The two men dropped on their knees to the ground.

Looking at the graves Tom dug and finished over, as well as the two stakes upright in the meadow's soil, Pall began his eulogy, "I did not know either Alicia or Mary long. But the time I spent with them is a gift of eternity. We became family together. And, as a result, became more than precious to me. I know that you, Lord, look upon them as being beyond value. As members of your family, I ask that you take them into your dwelling place and soothe their tears and let them rest in the peace of your arms. Pray provide us, the ones left behind in this place of strife, the grace to go on to honor their memory in the good we can do for others."

"Thank you, Pall," Tom said softly.

Myra gave Pall a hug and a pat on one of his shoulders.

The men stood up and stared at the graves, at the meadow around them and at the copper beech tree.

With Myra between them holding each of their hands, they walked back to the wagon. They stood under the tree with their hands held together, looking at it with wonder.

In a steady, small voice, Myra said to the copper beech, "Thank you, Sentinel, for saving us. Please take good care of my Ma Alicia and my sister Mary."

The tree cast its light steadily around them.

"I'm for hitching up the horses and getting back on the road," Tom said. "I don't think I can stay here much longer. If I don't go now, I may never be able to leave here."

"Okay, Tom," responded Pall. "Give me a rope when we're all set to go. Tie it to me and the front hitch to the team and I'll go on ahead on the road in front of the horses to make sure it's good for them to go over."

"Take one of the lanterns. I'll light it now from the fire we still got going. You can use it to help you see where you'll be walking," Tom advised.

"The tree's light and then the partial light from the moon will help us guide our way, too," Pall offered as reasons to get back on the road to Gullswater.

There was not much to stow back up in the wagon. Most of it was already packed. The team was hitched. They secured the fire, putting it out thoroughly. Tom put Myra on the wagon. He took the reins in his hands, and with Pall's help, they led the horses and wagon back onto the road.

Just before Pall was in place to lead the team down the road, he looked back at the tree glowing in all its glory in the field.

"Thank you," he said to it.

297

CHAPTER TWO

Pall had been leading the horses, Tom and Alicia, on the Gullswater Road for almost three hours without any incident. The dirt road was well built. There was a crude camber to it that helped spread rainwater to either side, and despite the recent rains, the surface, for the most part was smooth and uniform. There were places, particularly where the roadbed consisted of softer packed down soil, in which grooves were deeply scored from the constant traffic of other wagons passing over it. As there were no other travelers on the road this late at night, Tom had no problem letting the wagon slide into them and follow the marks until they ended.

Myra was sleeping on the small mattress in the wagon bed that both twins had used since the start of their journey toward a new life. Almost the moment after Tom and Pall started on the road in earnest toward Gullswater, she fell asleep against her father's side. They had stopped momentarily so that Tom could put his only remaining daughter left to him in a more comfortable position to rest.

Tom began nodding off. To prevent himself from falling asleep, he asked Pall to talk with him about anything, just so it would help the cooper stay awake and alert.

"Forgive me for asking you, then," Pall said. "What will you do now, Tom, especially after what just..." He could not finish his question and decided to ask, instead, "I'm sorry, I don't mean to be so rude, but will you still take the cooper's job in Gullswater?

Tom knew how difficult it was for Pall to ask him such a delicate question. Yet, he was glad for it to be asked of him; it helped him focus his attention on an answer he just did not have ready at the moment.

"I don't know, Pall, it's the first time I've put any thought to it. I think I'm in shock. And, I know for sure, Myra is too."

"I think you need more time to sort everything out," the young soldier suggested.

"Yes, I do. How long does it take, do you think, for folks like Myra and me to get a hold of what we're supposed to do?"

"I guess...." Pall thought out loud and paused to end his statement. He stopped walking and lifted the lantern high and then low to get a varied perspective on the road just ahead of him. Seeing nothing that caused him any concern or alarm, he started walking again.

"I guess everyone's different in how they take such an awful loss when they experience it," he said.

As Tom thought about what next to say, he remained alert to the noises the wagon was making and how it was moving over the road's surface. He paid heed to the creak and shifting of the leather reins, harnesses and tack on the horses, including the sound of their hoofs as they were placing them on the road's surface. The cooper was attentive to the mood of Tom and Alicia as they steadfastly pulled the big wagon after Pall's lead ahead of them.

"I think Myra and me'll take the cooper's job in Gullswater for now," Tom speculated. "I won't be breakin a promise after tellin the town fathers I would take the job. It would be wrong of me not to take it. Alicia would want me to work there. It'll force me to do somethin other than just thinkin about what happened. Maybe that's the best way goin about dealin with it until I have a firmer grasp on what we're doin."

"Sounds good, Tom," Pall said reassuringly to his friend.

They were quiet for a while. They traveled slowly, but steadily and safely for another half mile.

Tom asked Pall, "What will you do when we reach the town?"

"Like you and Myra, my friend, I don't know. Maybe I will just stay a bit as well to get my legs back under me. I'm trying to sort out who I am and where to go. I was hoping to meet a friend of mine, but I'm not sure he's been, or going to be, in Gullswater. I guess I'll see what happens once I'm there."

"If I can be of any help, Pall, just let me know. You're welcome to stay with Myra and me for the time."

"Thanks, Tom. I won't be staying long. I just pray that I will figure out what to do that's right for me."

They were quiet again. They traveled about another mile.

"Pall, I am quite spent and I think we need to call a halt. Let's find a decent place to stop off the side of the road and rest until daylight comes round again."

"Okay," Pall responded. "Sounds like a very good idea. I've gone through at least six candles. Let's stop the team and I'll go up and back down the road to see if there is a place where we can put up the wagon."

Pall brought the lead rope he was using back to Tom. He put a fresh candle in the night lantern and proceeded to go up ahead of the team on the left side of the roadway.

Tom watched the lantern's light almost fade away completely. He saw the light placed down onto the road. It remained in the same place for a few heartbeats. He saw that Pall had picked up the lantern again and crossed to the opposite side of the road, which was to Tom's right.

The lantern grew brighter as it started approaching the wagon. About two hundred or so feet away, Pall halted and then brought the light off to the side of the road. It was not long after he stopped that he came quickly back to the wagon.

Upon drawing even with the team of horses, Pall held Alicia's bridle. He patted her on her nose and talked softly to her. When he was done comforting her, he informed Tom, "There's an excellent place off the right side of the road just ahead for us to pull over and stay until we're better rested."

"Thanks, Pall: let's stop there for now. I don't want to press our luck anymore moving the team in the dark of the night."

Pall clicked at the horses, urging them on to the place that he had found for them to rest in from their labor of hauling the wagon. It was as if they sensed that the humans had made up their minds to stop being foolish by being on the road at night. They snorted and shook themselves in eagerness to get there.

Soon enough, they pulled off the road and found more than ample space to stop the wagon and to settle down for the remainder of the evening. They took care of the horses, made sure the brake was set on the wagon and began the process of getting ready for sleep.

Tom went in the back of the wagon and made his bed next to his daughter.

Pall pulled his mattress off of the wagon and placed it on a canvas underneath the wagon bed.

Soon, all three travelers, weary and spent from the torment of battle, the loss of loved ones and in a state of denial about the terrible pain and loneliness it was all bringing them, fell asleep into the quiet remains of the night.

CHAPTER THREE

Morning light failed to break their slumber. It was the creaking of a wagon passing by them in the road, and the whinnying of Alicia and Tom to the team leading it, that woke Myra. She, in turn, woke her father. Father and daughter proceeded to get up from their rest and in moving around in the wagon above him, Pall awoke as well.

They had plain and simple fare for breaking their fast. No fire was started and cooked over. They stayed in their same clothes.

Before Tom had anything to eat, he checked on his horses. He brushed them down after he fed them.

No one said much, until Myra, who was watching Pall eat his breakfast, addressed him politely, "Thanks, Pilgrim, for helping lead Da and me away in the dark from the tree of light."

"You're welcome, Myra," he responded.

"Weren't you scared being out in front of the wagon in the dark?" she asked him.

"No, I felt very safe," he assured her.

"Why did you feel safe?" she queried him again.

"Because you were in the wagon protecting us," he said with a straight face to her.

She looked closely at Pall to see if he was joking with her. When she could not tell if he was being serious or not, she giggled. "That's just silly: a three-year-old little girl makes you feel safe."

He nodded his head at her. "Yes, I felt safe because there was a three-year-old, little girl named Myra in the wagon whose love for her family is greater than anything I know in the whole wide world."

Myra tried puzzling out what Pall had just told her. She brightened at a thought she was entertaining and said, "Love can help people walk in the dark; right, Pall?"

"Yes, Myra, I could not have said it any better than you just did, little one," he said admiringly to her.

She kept her gaze on him as her eyes welled with tears. "Do you think the love me and Da have for Ma and Mary will help them walk in the dark, too?"

Pall glanced over at Tom who was listening closely to their conversation. "I think that if they were in the dark, they found their way because you and your Da's love helped them get home. I don't believe they're in the dark any longer."

Myra smiled at the young man. She leaned her head against her father's shoulder who was sitting by her side on the driver's bench to the wagon.

Pall had stood next to the wagon eating his food standing up. He had put the horses in their traces and they were ready to get back on the road to Gullswater.

"Thanks, Pall," Tom said, "that was a kindness you gave Myra and me, added to the fight you gave the beast last night. I will never forget what you did to help save us."

"You're welcome, Tom. I just wish I could have done more. Truly it was the Sentinel Tree that saved us all."

"Nevertheless," Tom insisted, "thank you."

Pall smiled back at the cooper, but it was a difficult one to share with his friend, especially when the young warrior was still very close to tears. "I think I'll walk a bit besides the wagon once we get going," Pall said softly.

They spent the rest of the day traveling towards Gullswater. It was late afternoon when they arrived there. They saw people single-mindedly going about their business. While they seemed unconcerned about the strangers in their midst, the citizens of Gullswater did not engage the newcomers with a greeting or even a direct look at them.

Pall was beginning to think that everyone in the town was just rude. Yet, to his pleasant surprise, when Tom asked for directions on how to get to the livery, the townspeople were very polite and cordial to him. Everyone Tom asked for directions gave him the information willingly and cheerfully.

Soon, Tom drove the team of Tom and Alicia to the front of the livery stable.

The livery was doing a brisk business. It was awhile before the proprietor came out of the stable to talk with them. When he found out that Tom was the cooper the town had sent for to fill the job, he became even more personable than before on first greeting them.

"Well," he said to Tom. "Welcome to Gullswater! My name's Lucas. I'll have my apprentice show you to the cooper's workshop. I think you'll like it. A portion of it's on the river, which is excellent for buyin and sellin what you make. Lots of room for a family like yours...."

Lucas stopped because he did not see any presence of a wife or mother to Myra in the wagon. Seeing the expressions of loss on their faces, he politely and quickly changed the topic. "Take a look around. The town's major merchant and craft guilds got together and pretty much set everythin up. The place should pretty much be ready to go. Go on over take a look around and let me know what you think of it, Tom."

"Thanks, Mr. Lucas," Tom said.

"Think nothing of it. Call me Lucas. Take your time over there. Get comfortable first. I'll come and see you round noontime tomorrow. Got to get goin now. We're fairly busy today. If I'm not around to spoil my customers, they get upset."

He waved goodbye to them and walked back into the gloom of the stable's wide flung, sliding doors.

Just as he disappeared inside a young boy came out and walked over to Tom seated in the driver's seat in the wagon. "I'm Lucas, Jr," he informed them, "but you can just call me Junior, that'll be good enough for me."

"Hello, Junior. I'm Tom. This here assistant to my right is Myra, and that's Pall—with a double L—yonder on the other side of the wagon."

"Hi, Junior!" Myra exclaimed. "You going to show us our new home?"

"Yes," he said beaming up at Myra who was sitting next to Tom.

"Hop aboard, Junior," Tom invited.

Without being asked twice, Junior jumped with great agility onto the wagon and soon was giving Tom directions on how to get to the cooper's workshop.

When they arrived at their long awaited destination, Junior jumped off the wagon saying,

"Gotta get back to the stable. The old man'll miss me and then there'll be trouble in it for me," he said to them just before he sprinted away back to see Lucas.

All three of them stayed on the wagon for a while. They stared at the workshop in front of them.

Tom looked at it with an appraising eye. He liked what he saw. With a deep sigh, he said, "May as well get the staves inside the iron hoop and finish raisin the barrel: let's go look at the place."

He stepped down from the wagon and helped Myra get off as well. After staring some more at the front of the building, he started walking to the front door. He stopped and looked back at the wagon. Seeing Pall next to it he said to him, "C'mon now. You're not gettin out of this. Please walk with Myra and me and see what kind of place we've been invited to live and work in."

Pall waved his hand at Tom, indicating that he heard and that he was complying with Tom's request. He joined up alongside them, and when they reached the front door, Tom opened it. Both men took each of Myra's hands and they lifted her through the door inside the front of the shop. Tom went in next with Pall following close behind him.

They spent the next hour looking around. Tom had to stop his assessment of the place because he wanted to take care of the horses. They were still patiently waiting outside at the front of the shop for someone to take care of them. After Tom and Pall unhitched the team, they brought them into a small stable next to the shop. The two men fed the horses and rubbed them down, praising them aloud for the incredible work they had done in bringing them to Gullswater.

Afterwards, they spent the remainder of the time getting most of the equipment and supplies off the wagon and into the cooper's work space.

Supper was brought over to them by Lora, Lucas' wife, and one of her older daughters. The women did not stay long. They hardly even introduced themselves before they were gone. The food was hearty, plentiful and filled their appetites more than adequately.

The three of them became quiet after finishing their evening's meal. They thought about what could have been and what Alicia might have said about the place, and how the two twins would have been running all over it, investigating every novel detail of their new home.

Pall shook off the torpor and gloom building around him. "Tom, I'm going to go get the mattress you've let me use and bring it in here. I think I'll get to rest early. I'm a lot more tired than I thought I was when I sat down to eat."

Tom nodded at Pall. "I think we'll do the same. We're gonna go upstairs to the loft and sleep there. See you in the mornin, Pall. Thanks for all your help. I couldn't have done it so gracefully without you."

"You're welcome, Tom. Good night."

Father and daughter left the room. Before leaving with Tom, Myra walked over to Pall and gave him a hug. "Good night, Pilgrim," she said. "I love you."

After they left the room, and after the little girl had expressed her love to him, the tears came. He did not remember falling asleep. There was aching grief, and then a void for about eight hours when he slept in the dark. No one seemed to be there to help him see if it was safe to be on the dream road he was now travelling.

CHAPTER FOUR

All three of them were awakened early the next morning because there was a knock at the front door. As Pall had slept in the front room over night, he answered the door. When he opened it he discovered that Junior was there with food to break their fast.

"That's really very thoughtful of your mother and father to put together this food for Tom and Myra," Pall told the boy. "And, thank you for bringing it over, too," he added.

Junior's face flushed. He gave a big grin at Pall and said, "Aw, it was easy to do. I just brought it over to them."

"True," Pall responded, "but it's the little things like what you just did for Tom and Myra that make the day seem to pass by easier."

Not knowing exactly what to say to Pall's comment, Junior bid goodbye and ran back over to the stables.

Pall closed the door and carried the food Junior had brought over to the Coopers to one of the smaller tables in the room. Just as he set it down on the table, Tom and Myra entered the room.

They exchanged greetings with one another. Pall told Tom about Lucas sending Junior over to the workshop with the food.

"I'll be goin over there soon," Tom informed Pall, "to let Lucas know that this place is just fine for my purposes. I'll have to ask his Lora about someone to help me take care of Myra when I'm workin. What about you, Pall, what are you goin to do now that you're in Gullswater?"

Pall looked at Tom and then studied his warrior's hands. He held them up in front of his chest. "They don't look like much, but all they've known is working at my father's forge and fighting."

"You're more than welcome to stay with us; you know that, right?" asked Tom.

"Yes, Tom, its kind and considerate of you to say so, and to invite me here to stay with you and Myra as well," he said.

"If you need work, I can certainly use your help here," as Tom gave this invitation to Pall, the cooper moved his hand over to his daughter's and held it tenderly.

The young soldier watched them for a moment and said, "I might need to stay here, no more than several days, I think. I need to find a friend of mine and I don't know if that is even possible to do. This morning, I thought I'd go into the town and ask around."

Tom nodded approval at Pall's words. "You know, Pall, how about askin Master Lucas how to go about findin your friend? Lucas sees a lot of people during the day and night and he knows even more of them in the town and surroundin area."

Pall stood up from the table. "Good idea, Tom. Think I will follow your advice. I guess I'll see you later on in the day. Good luck and God bless you this morning."

Pall went over and shook the cooper's hand. Myra gave him a hug, but he could see she was distracted and anxious to get back to exploring her new home more. He thought, *This is good that she has her mind set on wanting to learn more about her new place.*

He walked back to the front door. Before he let himself outside, he turned around to them and waved goodbye. They waved back and got up from the table to start their day.

Pall decided he would take Tom's advice and headed over to Lucas' stable. He took the time to absorb his new surroundings. There wasn't much to see, but he knew what he was not seeing and observing could make a huge difference on the success of his finding the bowman.

Regardless about what he thought was the townspeople's indifference to strangers earlier on the way into Gullswater, most of them nodded a faint hello to him as he went by them. He passed a variety of merchants and craftsmen's shops. There were more people, women, men and children, out on the town roads with him than he had suspected would be there this early in the day.

Arriving at the livery, he was surprised to see Lucas standing in front of the large, wooden sliding doors to his stable's entrance.

"Had an early rush of customers, n'now there's a lull. That'll go by soon enough. What can I do for you this mornin? Pall, isn't it?"

"Yes sir," Pall acknowledged. "Tom suggested I come over and see you about a friend of mine I have been looking for. He said you might be able to get me started."

"Okay, son, describe em to me. What's e do?"

Pall gave Savage's description, but did not tell him all the details of their association with one another.

"I'll ask around and make some inquiries," Lucas answered.

Pall thought the liveryman had avoided answering him directly.

Lucas, seeing Pall getting edgier in his presence, said, "Seems to me a big feller like that would be noticed by folks around here. Let you know later on in the afternoon what I find."

If anyone would have seen or heard of Savage being here, Pall thought, *it would be Lucas.*

315

"In the meantime, I'd check the Gullswater Tavern," Lucas had kept talking. "Most people stop there when they come to town."

"Thank you, Master Lucas," Pall said on the verge of sounding blatantly suspicious.

He asked the liveryman for the directions to the tavern. They were simple enough. Gullswater was not a very big place.

Lucas went back into the stables, letting out an audible sigh of relief when he was well inside his building.

The young warrior started walking towards the tavern, but he changed his mind and decided to walk around the town and get familiar with what was around him. He did not want to talk with anyone else about his search for Savage just yet, either. *Perhaps if I find out more about what's here, I'll get an idea what to do next*, he said to himself.

Pall spent the next several hours walking around the town, going into the shops and examining what was for sale. He watched people interacting with one another, listened as unobtrusively as he could to their conversations, and watched where they went and, if he could do so, what they did when they got there.

At one point in his observations he found himself along the riverfront. He noticed that almost all of the buildings here in this part of Gullswater had a pier or dock on the river from which they could conduct their separate tenants or owners' businesses by sending and receiving information and goods in either direction on the river. Most of the properties were in good condition.

Oddly enough, there was a collection of seven buildings next to one another that were in poor to rough order. He did not expect to find them in such a neglected state in the middle of the town's waterfront area. They were unkempt, even falling apart. He also observed that, whereas the well–ordered and well–kept buildings had foot traffic going in and out of them, these seven buildings that looked as though they should have already fallen down, had no one visible outside, or inside, them.

He only walked by them once, which was on the far side of the lane away from the frontage these buildings had onto the road. He did not want to attract any more attention than he had already done so. His instinct told him that he had been seen and observed from at least two of the buildings.

Noon came and went. Pall went out of the village limits, which was not far at all, and found a quiet, unoccupied spot on the river. He sat down next to it and became mesmerized by the swift flow of its current. He thought of the memories that had been returning to him from his former life. It all still seemed so disconnected to him. Yet, he did see that his life had been extraordinary for one so young, even miraculous. He thought of his parents, his life as a soldier and the battle that he had seemingly awoken from that started this journey to his being here, appropriately, on the Forgotten River.

"Maybe if I find transportation on this river," he stated aloud, "and I stay on it long enough, I'll either remember more, or lose what I have now, concerning my identity."

He wanted to find Savage, but he wanted also to find the elite troops that he had been such an integral part of for at least most of the time since he had left his father's forge. He recalled that Savage was with him when the Valravn attacked Pall and uttered the strange prophecy over him. At times, his arm still seemed to burn and itch from the strange bird's blood that fell upon it.

Most of all, though, and back in the deepest part of his mind, was the vision of a stunningly and beautiful looking, young woman with hazel green eyes, freckles and long red hair. Something happened to him when their eyes met. He could not explain the power of that connection. It seemed to offer a combination of promise and of peril that he did not want to think about anymore, regardless of his opposite yearning to explore these feelings further and to learn more about her as well.

The soldiers were calling her "Evangel;" *there must be some people around here who have heard about this strange woman in armor like mine.*

He also thought about the moments when he was deeply in contact with God and the miracles that happened to him when the Lord touched him, or when he touched the Lord. The memory of the battle with his young companions against the elite Aeonian veterans was a memory that had just recently resurfaced in his mind. Praying for the life of Captain Martains and seeing him revive and all those who were still alive do so as well, despite the severity of their wounds, still perplexed and awed him. He could not deny that these strange, yet wonderful, moments happened. In addition, his contact with the Herald, with the death ship, with his connection to the sword and its connection with him and his contact and battle with Ünger, all made him see that something behind these events was pulling at him very powerfully. But the forces tugging on him for his attention were completely foreign to him. He could not clearly understand their relevance and meaning to who he was and what he was meant to do.

At one moment, he felt poised on the edge of a huge realization about what everything in his life amounted to for him. At the very next moment, he thought he was going to be lost in a quagmire of confusion and darkness. The deaths of Alicia and her daughter Mary were taking a very heavy toll on Pall. He had faced death, as well as sent many opponents into death's arms, but he could not come to grips with the murder of these two precious lives. He replayed the fight against Ünger underneath the Sentinel Tree in his mind. The coruscations of power that came out of the demon, the seemingly protective power emanating from the tree that eventually took the beast's life away from it, and the power pouring out of the young man and the sword, overwhelmed his logic.

Either it's something that doesn't make sense, or is irrational, or it's a level of rational action that I have never considered before now.

Pall shook his head in consternation. There were just too many factors to consider.

He looked up at where the sun stood in the sky. He saw that from its angle where he was observing it, early afternoon was well upon him. He got up on his feet and walked away from the river. He bent his steps toward the tavern, thinking that people must be working up an appetite and a thirst that could best be quenched and appeased at the Gullswater Tavern at this time of day.

Entering the village once more he reflected to himself, *I need to find John Savage. He has the answers to many of my questions.*

End of *THE PENITENT – PART III*, **excerpt.**

ABOUT THE AUTHOR

A. Keith Carreiro earned his master's and doctoral degrees from Harvard Graduate School of Education, with the sequential help and guidance of three advisors, Dr. Vernon A. Howard, Dr. Donald W. Oliver and Professor Emeritus, Dr. Israel Scheffler. Keith's academic focus, including his ongoing research agenda, centers upon philosophically examining how creativity and critical thinking are acquired, learned, utilized and practiced in the performing arts. He has taken his findings and applied them to the professional development of educational practitioners and other creative artists.

Earlier in his teaching career he was a professor of educational foundations, teaching graduate students of education at universities in Vermont, Florida, Arizona, and Pennsylvania. He currently teaches as an adjunct professor of English at Bridgewater State University, as well as teaching English, philosophy, humanities and public speaking courses at Bristol Community College.

His research on creativity and critical thinking is based upon his experience in learning and performing on the classical guitar. He started studying this instrument at the age of four with Maestro Joseph Raposo, Sr., and took lessons with him until the age of 17. Keith also studied music theory and composition with Maestro José da Costa of New Bedford, and classical guitar with Robert Paul "Bob" Sullivan of the New England Conservatory of Music.

In 1973 at Ithaca College, he attended a master class workshop conducted by Miguel Ablóniz of Milan, Italy. Ablóniz' knowledge about technique and aesthetics attained a worldwide influence about the nature of guitar practice and performance. Maestro Andrés Segovia considered Ablóniz to be one of the world's most esteemed classical guitar teachers.

During the 70s, Keith performed his music and selections from the classical guitar repertoire throughout North and South America. He had many opportunities to play with a wide variety of musicians, composers, singer/songwriters, choreographers, theater directors, performers and conductors.

Due to his love of family, he has seen his fervor for history, as well as his passion for wondering about the future, deepen dramatically.

He lives in Swansea, Massachusetts and has six children and 13 grandchildren. He belongs to an eighty-five-pound golden retriever and an impish Calico cat.

59426927R10188

Made in the USA
Middletown, DE
11 August 2019